We Were Us

Heather Diemer

Don't be afraid to fall in love

Heather Diemer

We Were Us
Copyright 2014 Heather Diemer
First Edition
Cover Design by Cover to Cover Designs

DEDICATION

For You

CHAPTER ONE

It hadn't changed. The town. It had been almost a year and a half and the same sleepy sky stretched over the low, flat-roofed buildings that made up the main street of Riverview, Kansas. The sun blazed hot, keeping shoppers in the stores for as long as possible before they dashed out to their next errand, or to their car to race home and out of the summer heat.

I had passed my old house on my way into town. Memories flooded my mind and not the good ones. My mother was known as the town harlot and drug dealer who sold them for sex more often than money, so one can only imagine what I saw and heard as a child living there. Growing up I heard men call me cute, then pretty, then beautiful, and then said "just wait until you're eighteen…" My mother also tried to get me to do her business for her. She'd make me answer the door when she was too strung out to do it herself, and make the exchanges. As a kid, I didn't know I had a choice in the matter.

Eventually, I stopped doing her bidding and just left the house whenever the doorbell rang. I'd slip out through the back door and escape through the neighbor's yard. At first I would wander around town or down to the playground. But when I got older, I'd head down to the river and just sit, listening to the rippling sound as the current splashed over the river stones. The river became my solace, my hiding place, the one constant in my life that never let me down, even when I was forced to leave it.

One day, fifteen months ago, my mother was found in bed with the mayor. Both of them were passed out, high on something and naked. You'd think it would be a major thing to have something like that happen in such a small town, but it wasn't. The police were called, my mother was sent to jail, the mayor got off with just a slap on the wrist, and I was sent to live with my father and his wife five hours away in Brookhaven because I was technically still a minor. Three months from eighteen meant nothing in the eyes of the court system.

There I was, three months from my eighteenth birthday and three months from my high school graduation. I would be stuck living with my dad and his wife Linda, who hated me. To Linda, I was a reminder of my dad's unfaithfulness. I was the result of a one night stand between my parents while he was passing through Riverview. Paternity tests proved I was his. Of course my dad knew about what my mother did for a living, if you could call it that, and he tried to get custody of me, but Linda didn't want me, and my mom didn't want to give me up.

I sighed heavily and pushed all the bad memories as far back in my mind as they would go. I hadn't liked them the first time they'd happened and I didn't want to relive them over and over again in my head. I knew stepping into that house would bring forth more vivid memories, so why think about them before I actually had to face the reality of them in person?

I pulled into the parking lot of the tiny grocery store and shut off the car. It took less than thirty seconds for the midday heat to infiltrate the car after the air conditioner quit. I looked into the rear view mirror. I'd packed my car so tight with stuff I couldn't even see out that back window. Linda wouldn't allow me to store my stuff there for the summer--too much clutter--so I was forced to bring it all with me. I wasn't even completely sure anything else would fit, but I needed food, probably laundry soap at least, and there was no way I was setting foot inside the local diner. News of my arrival would flash through town before the waitress could get me a glass of water. I was hoping to sneak in and out of Miller's Market undetected.

I took a deep breath and opened the car door into the blazing heat and hurried across the black top parking lot. The bell tinkled and a blast of refreshingly cool air hit me when I opened the door.

"Good Lord Jesus, it's hot," I muttered to myself.

I'd barely taken two steps into the store when I heard my name. "Jenna? Jenna Mitchell? Is that you?" I turned to see who it was but I knew before I laid eyes on her who it was.

Lauren Marlow sat behind the checkout counter snapping her gum and twirling her long curly blonde hair around her fingers. She had a Cosmopolitan magazine open in front of her and her face was scrunched up questioningly, accentuating her stubby pig-like nose even more. Lauren was a nice person, she just didn't know how to keep her mouth shut.

"Hey Lauren," I said warily. She sat up straight on the stool she was leaning against and adjusted the ugly blue employee vest she wore.

Lauren's mother, Cindy, was the town gossip. She usually parked herself up at the Town and Country Diner and people watched all day. Nothing went on in this town that Cindy didn't know about. I'm sure Lauren had followed in her footsteps, being as she was the gossip of our high school, which meant everyone would know I was back in town.

"Well, what are you doing back here?" Lauren eyed me suspiciously.

I didn't feel like I needed to explain myself to Lauren, but I did. "I just came back for the summer. You know, break from school and all." I continued.

"Are you still in high school?" She feigned curiosity, but I knew what she was really asking. One of the rumors about me back then was that I was sleeping with my teachers to get good grades. Not true. I worked hard and earned my A's. I wasn't like my mother and I wanted out of this town to prove that.

"No. I just finished my freshman year in college." I punched back. I was getting annoyed with her questions. I hadn't just driven five hours to be interrogated within the first five minutes of being here.

"Is that right? Well, I'll be darned." She sat back on her stool and looked off behind me like she was contemplating something. I waited for her to say something more, and when she didn't look back to me, I took it to mean that we were done talking. Thank God.

"Yeah, well I need to get some things so," I trailed off and turned to go find food.

"Ooofff," I exclaimed as I ran into someone. I lost my balance and was about to hit the floor when a huge arm snaked around my waist to steady me. He pulled me into him so I was pressed up close to his chest. My left hand was pinned to my side and touching his jeaned leg, and my right hand was pressed into his toned chest. He smelled sweet and woody, a little sweaty and of the outdoors. I attempted to unpin my arm so I could free myself from this random guy and be on my way, but I stopped short when I heard him say my name.

"Jenna," came a smooth deep voice I recognized immediately.

Of all the people in this town I could have run into on my first day here, Josh Riley was the one I wanted to avoid the most. Even more so than Lauren or her mom. I heard Lauren flip a page of her magazine but I was pretty sure she wasn't reading it. In fact, I could feel her eyes boring holes into the back of my head.

Josh and I had a twelve year history of friendship that turned into a relationship, but ended abruptly and left my heart shattered. I'd shared with him my whole life. He'd been my rock when things were bad with my mom. We just had this connection that I thought was unbreakable, but one day he just decided I wasn't worth his time, and ended it. I thought I was in love with him, and I thought he loved me, but I was wrong.

I did not want to look at Josh, I wasn't ready to see him yet, but here I was not five minutes had passed since I'd arrived and I was already wrapped up in his arms. Being in his arms brought back all the memories I'd tried so hard to forget over this past year. Karma was not on my side today. Could I not just be in town for a day before I saw everyone?

"Um, you can let go of me now," I said when I'd come to my senses.

I glanced up at him. His stormy blue eyes were exactly as I remember them, cool but inviting. I searched his familiar face and found that a year and a half had changed him. He seemed taller than I remembered and more rugged. He'd lost the baby face I remembered and now sported rough stubble on his square jaw. His blond hair was shaggy around his ears and bleached by the sun that told me he worked outside. Probably at the Miller's farm.

"Josh," I said when he still hadn't let go, although I wasn't going to complain. Being back in his arms, even accidently made me feel like I was sixteen again. I'd practically been in love with him my entire life and the last year and a half had not damaged my memory of him. I couldn't say I wasn't sad when he finally did release me. He stepped back from me and allowed me to straighten my shirt and hair.

"What are you doing here?" I asked stupidly.

"Milk," he said simply, raising his arm up to show off the two gallons he held in one hand. He didn't take his eyes off me though, I didn't take mine off him.

"You look good." I said stupidly again. What was wrong with me?

"How's your mom, Jenna?" *Shut up, Lauren*, I wanted to scream.

Josh continued to stare at me until I became self-conscious. Did I have something on my face? I probably smelled bad after the long drive. Even with my air conditioning on full blast, it was hot in my tiny car. I probably looked like crap anyway. I had driven from my dad's in cut off jean shorts and a light blue tank top. I'd tossed my long hair into a messy bun to keep it off my neck.

"Umm, I don't know Lauren. She's still in jail," I shot back to her and gave her a mean sideways glance.

"Oh well, I just figured I'd ask," she said more to herself than to me.

Lauren went back to pretending to read her Cosmo, and I looked back at Josh.

"It's good to see you again Jenna." Josh finally spoke.

"Yeah, um, you too. See you around." Josh's eyes widened at my statement.

"You're staying?" he sounded all panicky.

"Yes, for the summer. I'm off from school. College."

"Where are you staying?"

"At my old house."

"Oh. When do you go back?" He sounded hesitant and worried at the same time.

Really? I'd just gotten here and he was already asking when I was leaving.

"Uh, at the end of August."

"Oh, ok."

We stood facing each other for a second longer than

necessary.

"Ok then. Enjoy your milk, and I'll see you around." With that, I snuck around him and headed down the closest aisle. I quickly found laundry soap, peanut butter and jelly and some bread and Ramen noodles. I decided to come back later for the cleaning supplies I knew I needed because I just wanted to get out of the store. By the time I got what I needed and was back at the counter, Josh was gone.

I quickly paid Lauren and left before she could ask any more questions. I sat in my car and relived everything that had just happened. Lauren knew I was here, which meant that the whole town would soon know. Josh knew I was here. I didn't know what that meant. It just felt good to be close to him again, but I couldn't let old feelings like that in again. Josh and I were done a long time ago. He was with Michelle now, at least I thought he still was. They could have broken up at some point. I guess I'd find out if I saw Michelle.

I threw the car in reverse and pulled slowly out onto Main Street. I can't remember if this was actually Main Street or if it was just called that because it was the main street through town. I looked for a street sign, but they were all missing. Not surprising. The kids in this town had nothing better to do than to be vandals.

Instead of going to the house, I headed down Main Street and out of town to my sanctuary, the river; a place I went when things were bad at my house with my mother. I usually walked there so I'd cut across the fields, winding my way through the corn stalks, creating my own personal maze. It felt like a secret mission only I knew how to complete.

I pulled off on the side of the road and looked out over the fields. The corn was only knee high and nowhere near tall enough for a secret mission. I sighed and turned back onto the road. I didn't feel like walking across a field in one hundred degree weather so I turned right at the next dirt road and took the easy way. I crossed Crystal Springs Bridge and parked on the side of the road. A wide, flat, muddy piece of land stretched before me and faded into the waters of the river.

During the summer, locals would host parties out here. They'd back their trucks up to the water and sit on the tailgates and drink, smoke, or whatever all night. Usually there was a bonfire on the other side of the river. I'd gone to a couple the last summer I was here but I never stayed long. Drinking and smoking weren't really my thing and neither were crowds.

I stepped out of my car into the heat again and made my way across the muddy embankment. I slipped off my flip flops and walked right into the cool water. I wished I wasn't wearing jean shorts right now, because it would feel good on this hot day to slip beneath the surface. Instead, I waded out until the water was about mid-thigh and just stood there, taking in the scenery.

On my side of the river, the water met the bank evenly so you could easily wade into the water, but on the other side, the flat embankment dropped off into six feet of water. Willow trees jutted out from the mud, clinging to the bank, digging the roots deep into the ground. One willow tree seemed to rise up out of the water, it's thin, wispy branches fell like an umbrella over the water. There was a small flat piece of ground that had been cleared a long time ago that held the bonfires during the summer. Blackened pieces of wood and sticks littered the ground, evidence that there had been a party recently, probably the seniors after graduation.

I skimmed the water with my fingertips and glanced to my left. If you followed the river from Riverside, you'd eventually end up in Brookhaven where my dad lived, and where I attended college. There, the river was deep and wide. Ferries took you across it, and fishermen fished on boats, not just off the banks. At night, the lights of the small city reflected off the dark waters and the amusement park lit up the Pier. A far cry from the humble trickle I stood in now.

I looked down through the crystal clear water to my feet and wiggled my toes. In Brookhaven, you couldn't see the bottom. I thought of my roommate Stefani and my best friend Andrew. The three of us had met our first day at BCC and something just clicked. I was grateful for people who didn't know my past and were only concerned with our future together as friends. Andrew was two years ahead of us, and had been our tour guide for that day. Stefani had a crush on him, but it was me he was interested in.

Stef moved on and found another boy and by the end of the school year, the four of us had formed a strange Breakfast Club-type bond and did everything together.

I sighed heavily at my thoughts. I had originally planned to stay in Brookhaven for the summer, but Linda had other plans. She was taking her kids to Florida on vacation and I wasn't welcome. Andrew had offered to let me crash at his apartment, but the two of us hadn't crossed any kind of intimacy line beyond kissing so I wasn't sure I wanted to spend the summer in such close quarters, especially if I wasn't completely sure of my feelings for him. I'd only had one serious boyfriend, Josh, and he'd broken my heart, but I felt this pull, this need to come back to Riverview one last time.

I needed closure on this part of my life. I needed to come back here to clean out the house so Dad could sell it, I needed to see Michelle and tell her how much I missed her and loved her and find out how she'd been for the past year, and I felt the need to see Josh in some capacity. I had seen him in the grocery store, and he seemed to have moved on from me, so I guess it was just the house and Michelle that I needed.

I turned and waded back out of the river, the water evaporated from my legs as soon as I was out. The coolness of the water hadn't really done anything to stave off the heat of the Midwest summer day. I hopped into my old trusty Honda Civic and set off back into town and to my childhood home. I wasn't sure what to expect, but I didn't have many fond memories there.

CHAPTER TWO

I rolled in over the gravel drive in front of the house around 2:00 and parked my car under the enormous oak tree that stood at the edge of the front yard. I'd always thought it was an odd place to put a tree. Its roots had grown up through the ground and through the cement of the sidewalk.

The old yellow house sat back from the road a little way, hidden by two even older oak trees. There was a red, wooden wrap around porch with tricky, stone steps leading up to it. You had to hop the second stair or risk breaking your ankle. The heavy oak front door stood timelessly guarding the house against intruders. Not that anyone would think to break into this house. It was mostly empty anyway.

I flicked the lights on after unlocking the door. *Good*, I thought, Dad was able to get the electricity back on. The air conditioning was off and it was boiling hot inside. The pungent smell of stale cigarette smoke lingered so I threw open the windows on my way to the thermostat. It was okay to crank the A/C with the windows open while it's 102 degrees out right? Whatever.

I walked through the house, taking survey of what needed to be done. The house was exactly how I'd left it, right down to the pair of socks I'd tossed on the couch that day after I'd come home from school. I needed to clean for sure. It had been empty for over a year now, and dust had settled on every surface. The living room was sparsely furnished, boasting just one shabby couch and an even shabbier TV stand. And when I said shabby, I didn't mean shabby chic. I turned into the bathroom, running my fingers across every dusty surface along the way. I could barely make out my reflection in the dust-covered mirror. I swiped my hand across the mirror throwing huge globs of dust and dirt into the air and tangling cobwebs into my fingers. I turned the faucet on but brown water spurted out. Gross, so I just wiped the webs on my pants instead. I decided to let the water run while I wandered through the rest of the house. I found my way to the kitchen and turned on the water there too as well as starting the washing machine, letting it run through a cycle before I started a load of laundry later. I put away what little food I'd purchased at the store and made mental notes of what more I needed: soap of every kind, bleach.

I saved the bedrooms for last. I ignored my mother's and headed straight back to mine. It was the same, just dusty. Knick-knacks covered every inch of the massive white dresser, a corkboard on the wall covered with all mementos of a life I'd left behind. Pictures of Michelle and I smiled back at me from every photo. There were a few of Josh, too. He was her boyfriend now, as far as I knew, but he was mine first. I cringed at the memories, but reminded myself I wasn't here to regain social status. I was here to live out the summer, quietly, clean out that house, and then go back to school in the fall. My phone vibrated in my pocket breaking me out of my depressing state of mind.

"Hello," I answered without looking at the caller ID.

"Hey Sweetheart, it's Dad. I just wanted to make sure you got home okay? Well back to Riverview I mean."

My dad was an amazing father for the situation we'd been dealt. He'd always felt badly about me not being able to live with him, and when Linda got after me about silly things, he told me to just ignore her. I was a living, breathing slap in her face, so she went out of her way to be rude to me. I didn't take it personally, I'd feel the same way if I were in her situation.

"Yeah. I just walked into the house. It's dirty." I added.

"Do you need anything? Do you need to stay somewhere else tonight?"

"No, I have the card you gave me and I'll go to the store again tomorrow morning."

"Okay. Use as much as you need. This is your account, Linda doesn't know about it. I know you are eighteen and I don't have to pay child support anymore, but you're a good kid and you've worked hard for what you do have. You deserve more."

"Thanks Dad. I'll call you later, okay?"

"Okay Sweetheart."

I hung up the phone and looked around my old room. I found

an empty shoebox and started tossing everything from my dresser into it. I might as well start packing things up now. Besides, I didn't want the constant reminders of my old life. I was moving on, and remembering what was and what could have been wasn't what I needed.

I was unceremoniously dumping everything in the box, but I paused at a small glass unicorn figure. Its body was clear but its mane and tail were turquoise and it had creepy black glass eyes. Michelle had an identical one except hers had pink hair. She'd insisted that we buy these horrid things at a street fair to commemorate our last summer before our senior year. "We'll have a magical summer, and a magical senior year! And these will remind us," she said before I could object. I thought about calling her but I didn't have her number anymore. I didn't know if she still lived in Riverview or if she'd even want to see me, after all, her dad was the mayor, the one who had been sleeping with my mom and doing drugs with her. Basically the whole reason she was in jail and I had to leave. I left the little glass figurine on the dresser and finished clearing it off then moved on to the corkboard.

In the midst of memories of concerts, school plays, and events, my phone rang again. I assumed it was my dad, but when the deep sexy voice of Andrew came across I immediately straightened up and ran my fingers through my hair. Like he could see me, I scoffed to myself.

"Hey Andrew, what's up?"

"Nothing babe. Just making sure you got to Riverview alright."

"Yeah, I just got in. My house is a disaster." I sat on the edge of my bed.

"You should have just stayed with me," he laughed.

"Yeah well, I have stuff here I need to take care of." I said, picking mindlessly at the lint on the bedspread.

"I know, you said that. When will you be back?"

"Right before school starts again in September, maybe a couple of weeks before. Stef and I don't know if we want to do the dorms again or get an apartment."

"I see. Well call me anytime. I miss you already." He sounded sad and pouty. I didn't know if he was being real, or over exaggerating.

"I miss you too, Andrew," I smiled. He always made me smile.

With that I hung up. I really did miss Andrew. He was funny and handsome. Okay, hot. He was tall, and dark. His eyes were brown and I normally hated brown eyes, but his reminded me of maple syrup when you held it up to the light, dark and warm. His hair was an unruly mess that my hands liked to get lost in. Not that they had had much of an opportunity to get lost though. Andrew and I had made out a few times, but our relationship was mostly platonic. I wasn't interested in a boyfriend my first year of college, and he had some broken past he wasn't interested in talking about. He was perfect for me, not into sharing.

After clearing my room of every high school memory and cleaning out the kitchen cabinets of expired canned and boxed foods, I washed all of the bedding in my room and plopped down on the bare mattress. I felt accomplished. I wasn't in high school anymore and I needed to clear out my mind and my physical space of everything that that reminded me of my past, so I could move forward with my life.

I moved next to the bathroom and found an old sponge and a bottle of bleach. Did bleach expire? I hoped not. I plugged the sink, filled it with water and bleach, and wiped down the bathroom the best I could. I figured I'd go over it again when I had better cleaning supplies.

I thought about my grocery store encounter with Josh while I cleaned. Fifteen months had done nothing to make me forget him. We had been friends since about second grade. There wasn't some monumental or clichéd reason we became friends, we just sort of gravitated toward each other. He was sympathetic about my mother and was my safe haven when I needed to get away from my house.

Josh was the one who had actually taken me to the river for the first time. We were probably eleven or twelve, and he took me down there one day when my mom was on a drugged-out tirade. We'd spent the day wading in the water trying to catch fish, skipping rocks and exploring up and down the banks. I'm pretty sure this was when I'd realized I was in love with him. I didn't even know what love was at the time, but I knew there was something between us.

When middle school happened, and girls and boys for some reason couldn't be friends anymore, neither of us cared. Michelle and I found each other, but still Josh and I remained close. Then one day I wasn't allowed at his house any more. I didn't know it at the time, but Josh's dad had slept with my mom. Even with our time together limited to school and when we could sneak out to the river, we still stayed close. He would call me in the middle of the night when he knew his mom would be asleep, and we'd still sneak off to the river any chance we could get.

I sighed at all the memories flooding my system, and sat down on the toilet seat, tossing the old sponge into the bathtub. The sun was setting so I guessed I'd been cleaning for close to six hours. I was done for the day, mentally, emotionally, and physically.

I left the bathroom and thought about lounging on the couch to read, but one glance at the dirty couch and I knew there was no way in hell I was sitting on it and there was no way it was staying in this house. I sighed again and propped the front door open. I pushed the full-sized couch onto the porch and tipped it over down the stairs, then dragged it out to the curb. I hoped that trash day was soon. The living room was bare now. Only the television and stand remained.

I vacuumed and then decided to quit for the day. I'd need to go to the store again tomorrow for more supplies and food. I didn't scrub the fridge out yet, I wasn't even sure I wanted to. I'd save that for another day. Or never. I could probably live off of peanut butter and jellies all summer. I remade the bed after pulling everything out of the dryer, grabbed a book, and tried to read. I was so emotionally and physically exhausted, I'd fallen asleep before I had finished the first page.

CHAPTER THREE

I woke up the next morning drenched in sweat with the pages of my book stuck to my skin. I peeled the covers back and rolled out of bed. I'd left the windows open all night and the air conditioning did nothing to counter the heat from outside. I didn't even think the temperature had dropped below eighty overnight. I quickly shut all the windows and cranked the thermostat. By the time I got out of the shower, the house had cooled down, but the cigarette smell still lingered. I would just have to deal with that.

I slipped on a pair of denim capri pants and a purple tank top and headed out the door to Miller's Market again. This time I had a list so it shouldn't take me long. In and out, no talking to anyone unnecessarily, and no bumping into people.

Lauren was behind the counter again, but I hurried past her without saying a word and snagged a cart on my way to the soap aisle. Once I'd stocked myself up on everything from sponges and mops, to every kind of spray cleaner ever made, I rounded the corner to the next aisle to find more food and rammed my cart into another. Didn't I just tell myself not to bump into anyone?

"Sorry," I said quietly, not looking up to see who it was.

"Jenna Mitchell?" Came a cold sneer. My whole body sagged in response to the voice. Mayor Banks. The reason I was forced to leave Riverview, my best friend's father, and the person I most wanted to avoid. Was there a secret entrance to this store somewhere that let through everyone I didn't want to see?

"Mr. Banks," I said quietly. I didn't even know what else to say.

"What are you doing here?" I looked up at him finally, his cool, unwelcoming face wiped my brain of anything I was thinking about saying. He glared down at me with expressionless brown eyes.

"I, um, I'm buying some cleaning supplies?" I finally managed and it turned into a question.

He continued to stare down at me intimidatingly and I pulled back away from him in an attempt to put as much distance between us as possible. I wanted to get away from him, but his cart and a display of canned beans were blocking my way around.

"I see, well I hope you aren't planning on staying around here long."

"I'm staying the summer," I said too quickly. I wondered why I was volunteering information to this man.

"You're what?" he asked scathingly.

I didn't respond. I didn't want to say anymore to him. I wanted to get out of the store and never come back. This place was cursed for me. I was naïve to think that I could spend the summer here undetected.

"Well you aren't welcome here, young lady. Don't try to worm your way back into this town's good graces. No one wants you, especially not anyone from my family."

"I," I squeaked.

"Don't try to contact Michelle either. You've done enough damage to my family as it is. There's no use in making it worse for everyone."

I lost the rest of my words at that. Tears threatened behind my eyes, but I refused to let this man get to me. Even more, I refused to let him see how much he was getting to me. I took a deep breath, swallowed the lump in my throat, and squeezed my cart between his and the canned beans and hurried off down the aisle. Thankfully, it was an aisle I needed.

I lingered in the back of the store for twenty minutes to make sure I wouldn't meet the mayor at the checkout counter. Lauren was the only person up there and I wanted to avoid more interactions with him. Lauren must have heard our entire exchange because she didn't say a word to me while she rang up my items. Instead, she kept looking at me with a sorrowful look on her face. She started to say something several times, but stopped herself.

"Spit it out Lauren," I said. I was angry and trying not to cry.

"He's a jerk," she said quickly.

"Yeah," I didn't want to cry in front of Lauren.

"You don't have to take shit from him. Just ignore it. He's about to get kicked out of office anyway and his wife is going to divorce him. That's what I hear anyway."

"Well good, he deserves it."

"Yeah."

"Thanks Lauren," I said.

Maybe Lauren wasn't so bad after all. She was never directly mean to me in high school and she wasn't being rude about me being back now. I felt like I should give her a chance. I could use at least one friend in this town.

"If you need anything, you know where to find me," Lauren said after she'd bagged up my purchases.

"Thanks," I said to her again.

When I got home, I just dropped the bags on the living room floor, sat down in the middle of the floor and cried. I never imagined it would be this emotional coming back here. All the old feelings I had for Josh, the memories in this house, and now being all but forbidden to see Michelle. She was my best friend and the one person I actually wanted to see. Along with Josh, she had been there for me during the times when my mom was being crazy. I'd stay the night at her house for days, I told her everything, we'd even made plans for after graduation to go to college together and be roommates, and we'd even planned a trip to Europe.

In the middle of my wallowing, someone knocked on the front door. A flash of possibilities of who it could be crossed my mind. Lauren's gossip had had time to make its rounds so it really could be anyone. More than likely a nosey neighbor wondering why I was back and if my mom was here. Chances were they were looking for something only she could provide. I stood frozen in my seated position on the floor, but I knew that whoever it was had already seen me. The knock came again along with a voice.

"Jenna, it's me. Open the door."

I scrambled to my feet and wiped my tears before I turned around to answer the door. What the heck was Josh doing here? I smoothed my hair the best I could.

I opened the door and there stood Josh. Sweat dripped from his forehead and chin and his shirt was damp, but I saw why. Behind him was the most hideous couch I'd ever seen. It was burnt orange, with pea green and yellow flowers all over it. I looked from the couch to Josh and back to the couch again. Confusion played on my face.

"I saw the couch outside your house last night, so I brought you a new one." Josh had a huge grin on his face as if he had just saved the world or something.

"Um, thank you," I said and moved out of the way and watched as he dragged the monstrosity in.

"Where do you want it?" he said straining.

"Um, just against that wall is fine," I said and pointed to the wall opposite the television.

Josh positioned the couch against the wall and we both stood back to admire its hideousness. The puke green really stood out against the orange. I think Josh's definition of 'new' was different from mine. I think they stopped making this pattern in 1972.

"Thank you so much. How much do I owe you for it?" I could be polite for free stuff.

"Nothing," he said pushing the couch into place.

"I have money Josh," I said. "And I obtained it legally."

Josh whipped around and stared at me. He ran his fingers through his sweat dampened hair and down over his face then wiped it on his jeans. You'd think I'd find that a little disgusting, but really I just wanted to run my hands through his hair as well. I hadn't really stopped thinking about our interaction at the grocery store.

"What's that supposed to mean?"

"Please. I know what people in this town think of me. I'm not here to follow in my mother's footsteps. I'm in college now. I'm just not welcome at my dad's house in Brookhaven."

"I know you're not like her Jen. I know."

"Okay." I didn't know what else to say.

"Do you have food?" he asked.

"Yep, living on caviar and lobster." Sarcasm at its finest.

Josh laughed at this then seemed to lose his words. He looked around the living room at everything but me.

"Let me take you out this weekend," he said finally. He placed his hands on his hips matter of factually, like he knew I'd just say yes without hesitation.

I was completely caught off guard by this. Why in the world would Josh want to take me out? We had ended a long time ago and last I knew he was still with Michelle.

"What about Michelle?" I blurted out.

Josh balked at my question and grimaced. His reaction made me wonder if something had happened to her.

"I'm not with Michelle."

"I'm sorry. Is everything okay?"

"Yeah, why do you ask?" he said. He shifted uncomfortably and ran his fingers through his hair again.

"No reason. I ran into Mayor Banks at Miller's earlier today."

"Oh geez, how was that?"

"Awkward to the max. He told me specifically to stay away from Michelle."

Josh shifted again and looked at the ceiling, like really concentrated on the ugly, glittery popcorn mess above us.

"Are you sure everything is okay? What's going on?"

"Nothing, but if the mayor said not to go see her, then you probably shouldn't."

"Yeah, okay." I was confused as to why Josh was siding with the mayor, but maybe my mother had ruined things with their family more than I thought.

"So, do you want to have dinner with me?"

I paused, still thinking about Michelle. "Yeah, sure," I said finally.

"We could go to the city. There are a ton of places to eat there." His easy smile had returned and he visibly relaxed now that we weren't talking about Michelle.

"It's like an hour's drive though," I countered.

"We can catch up," he said enthusiastically.

"Okay sure."

We stood there awkwardly for a few seconds. I looked down and laughed.

"What's so funny?" he asked

"Nothing. Just you. You in my living room. You bringing me a couch. It's weird."

"Why?"

"I don't know."

I did know though. I was never able to bring friends over when my mom was here. The house was always a disaster and smelled of cigarettes and God knows what else. It was embarrassing and I kept Michelle and Josh away to avoid unnecessary interactions with my mother.

"Well, I need to clean out the fridge but I'm a little scared."

He laughed at that. "Why's that?"

"Because I don't know what's in there. I left quickly fifteen months ago and that meant leaving everything as it was. No one has been here since then."

"Well, I can help with that." He didn't even make a face at the possibility of the grossness that could be waiting behind the door.

I was taken aback by this.

"You want to help me clean out my disgusting fridge?"

"No, but I'm here now with nothing to do so I'll help."

"Far be it from me to turn down free labor. I was just going to make a peanut butter and jelly sandwich. Do you want one? Its new jelly, and not been in the fridge. It's probably okay since it's only been on the counter for one day." I was rambling but I really didn't know what to say to him.

"I think a peanut butter and jelly sandwich sounds great."

"I have Dr. Pepper."

"Even better."

The fridge wasn't as bad as I thought it would be. There wasn't much food in there to begin with. I mean, I'd fended for myself most days and lived on canned soup, boxed cereal, and macaroni and cheese. I honestly didn't know what my mother ate. She never cooked and I don't ever remember seeing her eat anything.

A couple hours later after tossing some moldy lunchmeat and a few indistinguishable plastic containers, we had cleaned out the fridge. Josh took the trash out for me. When he returned we stood awkwardly in the kitchen for a few minutes. I was done cleaning for the day and desperately needed a shower, but I also wanted to be with Josh some more. His close proximity brought up old memories and when he'd accidentally brush my arm with his, or touch me gently on the back as he scooted around me, I got all flushed and excited. Thank God I was pushed up inside the fridge so he couldn't see me. I half wondered if he was intentionally touching me.

"Well, I should probably get going," he said after we had finished.

"Yeah. I need to shower again," I said.

Josh shifted uncomfortably.

"I can't wait to see you again," he said.

"Really?" I was still a little baffled as to why he wanted to hang out with me after all this time.

"Yeah. I missed you Jenna. We were friends."

"Why?" I couldn't help myself.

"Geez, Jenna. I'm not like everyone else in this God forsaken town." He slammed his soda can down on the counter causing me to jump.

"Okay sorry," I said quietly.

Our conversation lulled. I stared out the kitchen window at the blindingly white afternoon sun. Maybe I should get some curtains. I thought about what else I needed to do for the house. I thought of any heavy lifting I might need done to keep Josh here longer, but there was nothing left to do. My mother's room remained untouched, for all I knew there was a homeless man holed up in there, or a band of feral cats.

"So what are your plans for the rest of the week?" he asked pulling me out of my daydream.

"Besides our plans, I don't really have any plans. I thought I would just lie around on my ugly new couch and read."

"You think it's ugly?" he genuinely looked hurt by this.

"Oh come on Josh. Look at it. It's atrocious."

"I'm sorry."

"Oh dude. I'm not complaining! I was just being funny."

"I see. Well, have fun reading."

We were almost to the door.

"I thought about going to see Michelle." She'd been on my mind the whole time he was here. I wanted to see her and tell her how sorry I was about my mom. I knew she wouldn't blame me.

She knew how my mom was. Michelle had sat through countless hours of my ranting about my mother. She never said anything rude about her, but she listened none the less, like a good friend should.

Something about the way her dad told me to stay away and the way Josh was acting told me something was up.

"No," he stopped suddenly.

"She dislikes me that much, huh?" Maybe I should just let it go. What my mother had done had probably destroyed their family, and I'd just be an unwelcome reminder of it all.

Josh visibly relaxed. "Yeah," he said, though his admission hurt a little.

"I guess I'll just hang out with you all summer then." I said half kidding.

"That would be great," he said enthusiastically.

I gave him a puzzled look but inside, I was leaping for joy. Josh's attitude toward me was not at all what I had imagined. I came back hoping to avoid him and expected the cold-shoulder if I did see him. It seemed as though he wanted to be around me, he did just ask me out, after all.

"Well okay then," I said.

"Okay. Well, I'll see you later then." And he left.

I flopped down on the ugly couch and thought about what had just happened. Josh asked me to dinner. Josh had said he wanted to hang out with me all summer. Josh wasn't with Michelle anymore. I rolled over onto my belly, which was almost impossible on this couch. It was soft and swallowed me in its thick cushions. Josh, wanted to hang out with me, I repeated to myself.

I stared at the TV. What would we even do? I wanted to keep a low profile while I was here, especially after my run in with the mayor. I wasn't here to cause trouble or follow in my mother's footsteps. I looked at the TV again, I wonder if I could call Dad and ask for cable. Or maybe internet, I had my laptop with me and a Netflix account.

The rest of the day wore on dully. My phone rang a few times but after seeing Josh, I wasn't interested in talking to Andrew. I needed a mind break, and answering my phone would just give me a headache. I wandered in and out of the rooms absently. Finally after a shower and another peanut butter sandwich, I settled on the bed to read.

The rest of the week was dull as well. Dad promised cable and internet by next week, until then I had my iPhone and books to keep me company. I drove down to the river one day just to think. I knew why I'd come back here, but I was still questioning myself. Did I come back to rekindle my relationship with Josh? Sure I missed what we had, but he had broken my heart. I really didn't have anywhere else to go this summer. I wasn't welcome at Dad and Linda's, but it's not like she forbade me to live there this summer. I just wasn't interested in being around her or her kids. When I'd asked Dad about staying in Riverview for the summer he was hesitant, but agreed.

I was unable to shake my interactions with Josh. I dreamt about him that night. Sometimes Andrew would be there too and I couldn't tell the two apart and they each got mad at me for missing the obvious. In real life they were two very different men. Josh was rugged and gritty. His sandy blond hair and baby blue eyes betrayed his harder side. Everyone in town loved Josh. He was never the football hero or the greatest student, but he was loyal, and kind and always ready and willing to help anyone in need. He'd grown up quickly though with just his mom to take care of him, he had started work out at the Miller's at an early age. Andrew on the other hand, was clean and refined. A city boy to the core. His dark hair and mysterious eyes lured me to him. A mystery for the most part, but he knew nothing of my past. I liked that the most about him.

CHAPTER FOUR

The day of my date with Josh was here. I hadn't thought about anything else since he'd asked me three days ago. I replayed every word of our conversation over and over again. I thought about every possible scenario that could happen on the date. What if he didn't show up? What if he changed his mind? What if we had nothing to talk about on the two hour drive there and back? What if he tried to kiss me? What if he didn't? That were a lot of what ifs', I mean, it wasn't like we'd never kissed. He was my first kiss, so it wasn't something I could easily forget.

We were at the river just sitting on the bank watching the water flow downstream. It was hot so we had our feet in the water and he'd just leaned over and kissed me. Just once. I was so caught off guard that I just sat there silently. We were twelve. We kissed a few other times while we dated in high school, but Josh and I didn't make the best couple. We tried, but it was too forced, like we were trying to save our friendship in the worst possible way.

I slept in until noon then fretted around the rest of the day being indecisive. I almost called him to cancel five different times, but finally I got in the shower, did my hair and makeup, and stood in front of my closet hating every outfit in it. It was just dinner with Josh, but I wanted to look nice. I wanted to impress him. I wanted to erase the old me, the sixteen year old me and make him see who I had become since leaving.

After multiple outfit changes I decided on a mid-thigh length, white cotton dress. It had thick straps and a deep V-neck with lace patterning all over. I'd originally bought it the summer before my senior year and planned to wear it to graduation. Michelle had bought the same one. We were going to match. I had worn it to my graduation; I wondered if she had worn it to hers. I tossed aside the white heels I'd worn with it that day in favor of my cowboy boots. I snagged a short denim vest and slid it over my shoulders. Shoot, I looked country. I shrugged out of the vest and grabbed a lace back cardigan instead.

I stood in front of the mirror for a bit longer, thinking of all the crazy things Michelle made me do. She really had the more outgoing personality. The cliché of the fiery redhead having a fiery personality was completely true in Michelle. Even though Michelle had a sister, Renee, Michelle insisted I was her true sister even though we looked nothing alike. We both stood at five feet seven inches, but while her hair was beautifully red, mine was boring, chestnut brown. Her vibrant green eyes offset her flawless fair skin. I, on the other hand, had 'wannabe' green eyes. Michelle said hazel was beautiful too, but I never believed her. I was jealous of her green eyes, and she was jealous of how easily I was able to get a tan.

She was the one who got me to try out for softball. Without her, I never would have gotten the scholarship to attend college. She was always coming up with hair-brained ideas about what we'd do after college. I, the sensible one, always said we would be roommates in the dorms, graduate together, then find jobs doing the same thing so we could be together forever. It was my attempt at holding onto the only person who'd ever been consistent in my life. She, on the other hand, wanted to rent a funky apartment downtown and paint it wild colors, and have sophisticated parties every weekend. I'm sure she cared less about graduating and jobs and more about perfecting our social lives in the big city of Brookhaven. She was ready to leave tiny Riverview behind and start new.

Once I was satisfied with my ensemble and hair do, I slumped on the couch and waited for Josh. The sun was low in the sky to the point where it would shine through the window at any moment. I had this game I made up when I was a kid to pass the time since we didn't have television. I'd stare out the window and count until the sun set low enough to shine through the window. Whatever number I got to was the number of days I'd have left in this house before someone would save me. Of course this as completely ridiculous. The timing of the setting sun had nothing to do with my life. But, in my preteen mind, it did. So I stared at the window lost in a game. Waiting for the sun, counting.

I looked past the trees and houses and could almost see the

roof of Michelle's house. I thought about going over there, but Josh's reaction to my idea, and Mayor Banks' threatening words, held me back. I missed her and I wanted to explain to her what had happened. I hoped she knew that I was sorry and that I had no idea my mother was sleeping with her father.

A soft knock startled me out of my trance. I'd lost count, but I think I'd gotten to five hundred and eighty-seven. I really hope I didn't have to wait five hundred and eighty-seven days for someone to save me.

I cursed under my breath and leapt to the door when I heard him knock again. There was Josh dressed in dark blue jeans, grey plaid shirt with light blue stripes that picked up the blue of his eyes.

His face twisted into a look of shock and pain when he saw me. I looked down at myself and stood there awkwardly while I tried to figure out what the cause of his reaction was.

"Umm…" I said and looked down at my boots.

"Where'd you get that dress?" he asked in an accusatory way.

"I bought it a couple years ago. I wore it for my high school graduation. Michelle has the same one. We were supposed to wear them together," I rambled on.

"Oh." he looked mildly relieved.

Wow. I thought this dress would get me a kiss at the end of the night. Instead, I get moody negative noncommittal, non-word reactions. I checked his face again, he still looked uncomfortable, but he managed a smile.

"Should I change?" I turned back into the house, fully ready to strip and find something less awkward to wear.

"No. It's fine, you're fine. You look fine."

Fine was not what I was looking for either.

"Okay." I grabbed my purse before heading out the door with Josh. He shuffled and coughed behind me while I locked the door. I turned back to him and was greeted with one of his patented grins. While most of Josh's friends on the football team had perfected the 'panty-dropping smile', Josh had somehow transcended beyond panty dropping straight to heart melting and swoon worthy. He was like a Disney prince or something. The

Beast after Belle breaks the spell. That was the smile I had wanted to see.

"I'm sorry. You look beautiful tonight. It's a beautiful dress."

Josh took my hand and led me out to his truck. My heart skipped a beat when he lifted me up into it. Why was I being such a girl right now? I'd thought of Josh non-stop for the whole week, I'd gone over every possible scenario that we could encounter. I did that so I wouldn't look like an idiot or say stupid things. But I was not prepared for the way I reacted to his touch. It wasn't like an electric shock or anything, more like white hot liquid pulsating from where he touched through my whole body.

We drove an hour into the city for dinner and we didn't say a word the entire time. It was silent and awkward. I watched him start to say something a dozen times then just cough and shift uncomfortably. Where was his confidence from the other day when he'd asked me out? Was it the dress that had thrown him off?

***

The restaurant was small and stuffy, the food was mediocre, the staff was downright awful, and we both knew it. Josh sent back his steak three times before it was done correctly. We weren't offered a discount, but we were given a coupon to come back again. Not likely. I felt bad that Josh had driven an hour for this.

"I'm sorry," he said as we were finishing our meal.

"It's fine. It was better than the peanut butter and jelly I would have had." We both laughed.

"So do you still play softball?" he asked breaking the silence

"Yeah, I do. I got a small scholarship for college even."

"Oh wow. That's great."

"Yeah. I was somewhat surprised. I mean, I only played one season at the school, but I had a great coach who really encouraged me."

"Well you were also really awesome. I remember going to your games."

The server handed us our check.

"You just went to see Michelle," I half teased.

"I went to see both of you," he retaliated.

I'd skirted around the subject of Michelle all dinner long, but he never alluded to anything.

"So how is Michelle?" I couldn't help it. I had to know.

Josh frowned as we stood up to leave. His face hardened into a grimace. Geez, was it that bad? Did she hate me with the wrath of a thousand moons?

"She's fine. But don't go see her." He opened the door and ushered me out into the parking lot.

I wanted to ask why he was so adamant about me not seeing her, but his stony expression made me stop. He didn't say anything more about it so I let it go. My heart sank a little though. I just wanted to tell her I was sorry.

"Well, she was better than me anyway."

Josh clicked the buttons on the keyfob and the truck doors unlocked. I opened the door and hopped in before he could do it for me. Not because I didn't want him to, I just wanted to do it myself.

"So are you in school too, Josh?" I asked after he'd gotten in too and started the engine.

"Yeah, I'm taking classes at the community college. Mostly Ag stuff for the farm."

"Well that's good."

"Yeah. The Millers want to hire me on full time when I graduate."

"That's great!"

"Yeah it is. Its great pay and I don't have to move."

"So you want to stay here forever then. In Riverview?"

"It's not so bad Jenna. For me it's not."

"For me it is," I said. And it was. I just couldn't see myself living here for the rest of my life, knowing how this town felt about me and my mother and how they'd treated us for years. No, I couldn't stay here. I was here to move on, not be held back.

"Yeah," he agreed.

The drive back home was quiet and boring. We'd lost our conversation once we left the restaurant. I gazed past my reflection in the window and found the Orion constellation and the Big Dipper, the only two constellations I knew. I wanted to get past this awkwardness with Josh. We never used to be this way. Even when we dated we still had great conversations and our time together was easy and not forced.

Soon it became a game for me to count down the mile markers. I knew we had to get to exit thirty-three before we were on the road to home and we were currently on eighteen.

"You might want to plug your nose." Josh said.

"Why's that?"

He didn't even need to answer, an overwhelming scent of rotting eggs, meat, and any other disgusting, rotting substance filled the car.

"Oh. My. God. Josh! I know we're friends, but you need to keep that kind of thing to yourself. That is not even something I want to hear or smell. God!" I gagged.

"What? No! Jenna. That wasn't me. I promise. You don't remember this?"

"Remember foul smells? No. I don't make a habit of committing those to memory."

"It's the natural gas refinery just off the highway. I can't believe you don't remember it and that you thought I was capable to creating that kind of smell. I'm hurt."

I looked over and him and his huge blue puppy dog eyes. He was really good at this face.

I gagged again before responding. "You're a guy, all guys are capable of that kind of smell. Besides, I don't know what you eat."

Josh just laughed.

"Gah," I said again.

Josh continued to laugh at my reaction to the smell as I gagged.

"What else am I forgetting about this place?" I asked when I'd recovered from the smell.

"Well, that crazy lady who lived down the street from you died."

"Aw, sad."

"Yeah, and that creepy history teacher finally got fired."

"Oh wow. Yeah. He was weird. He touched me a lot."

"That doesn't surprise me. He might be in jail right now because of *touching* students."

"Ha. He probably deserves it."

"Let's see, what else have you missed?"

I looked over at him smiling, but it quickly faded when I saw his expression. A frown replaced his easy smile.

"What is it?" I asked. I was a little concerned by his dramatic change in moods.

Josh shook his head as if to shake away the thoughts. "Nothing. I just thought of something I forgot for the farm." I could tell he was lying, but I let it go. I wasn't into fighting on our first date.

When we finally pulled into the driveway in front of my house, I was ready to get out of the truck. We hadn't talked for the last twenty minutes of the ride and it was getting awkward again. I didn't even know what had happened with the conversation, it just stopped.

Despite the abrupt end to our conversation, this date wasn't a total bust, but I hopped out of his truck before he even shut the engine off. I didn't want him to feel obligated to take the night any further. I'm not sure what I was even expecting.

I hurried up the steps to my porch and opened the screen door. Josh hustled after me and skipped up the steps catching my hand before I opened the main door. We were consumed in darkness because I'd forgotten to turn the porch light on. The headlights from his truck gave us some light; just barely enough to make out the sincere look on his face.

"Jenna, wait. I'm sorry this sucked. I was nervous."

"Really? Why?"

"Because it's you."

"What about me?" I asked.

"Just you, here, back in town. I missed you."

"Are you expecting me to put out or something? Because I'm not my mom."

"Uh, no. No! God Jenna. I don't see you like that. I just thought I'd never see you again and I didn't want things to end badly again." He looked a little horrified and then sad.

"We didn't end badly, Josh."

He stared at me silently. He was good at the silent thing. He stared a little longer than was comfortable, his eyes searching mine.

"Jenna I…" I didn't let him finish.

I had meant to go in for a kiss but at the last second chickened out. Instead I slipped my arms around his waist and pressed my cheek to his chest. The woody scent of his cologne invaded my nose, leaving me longing for more than just a hug. His hands moved around my back and tangled into my hair. I looked up at him still pressed against him. He wasn't looking at me, but staring off into the darkness. I rested my chin on his chest. He looked down at me and kissed my forehead. My mouth was jealous.

"Goodnight Jenna," he said softly in my ear.

I shivered. Did he know how much I still liked him? How much I still wanted him? I had barely been here a week and I was already falling back under his spell.

CHAPTER FIVE

Dad called me to tell me that someone would be out early next week to hook up the cable and internet. I loved him for doing this for me. I'd feel connected to the world again. Not that I minded being tucked away, happily oblivious to what was happening elsewhere, but I missed TV. I missed *Supernatural* and schmexy Dean Winchester. I could watch him all day. Sometimes I did.

He also mentioned that Mom had called him. She'd heard that I was back in Riverview and she wanted me to go see her. I rolled my eyes several times during that conversation. I really didn't want to to see her. I'd severed all ties with her the day I'd left, I hadn't written, called her, or contacted her in any way since then. He told me I really should, or at least go to the jail and change her contact number from his to mine. He was able to answer the phone this time, but didn't want to think about what might happen if Linda answered next time. That would have been catastrophic.

I threw on jeans and a white tank top, slipped into an old pair of silver flip-flops and headed to the county jail. I'd been there once. It was the day after she'd been caught with the mayor. I'd spent the night in protective custody at the police station after several hours of questioning. The social worker thought it would be good for me to visit one last time. It hadn't gone well. She had accused me of setting her up and said I was the real slut and drug dealer. Of course, no one believed her.

At one time, my mom had tried to be a good mom. Really. She'd provided for me the best she could. But I either became too much for her to deal with, or the drugs just took over every aspect of her life, that it made it impossible for her to think about anyone or anything else. When I turned sixteen, it had gotten ten times worse. At first, she wanted me to join her because apparently a mother/daughter team could make much more money. Of course, I said no. I was a good student and I actually wanted to attend college. I did not want her life or to be stuck in this small town forever.

After my refusal, she was bitter and nasty. She insulted me any and every time she saw me. My clothes, my hair, my body, school; anything was a target for her. Her words cut deep, but Michelle was my savior, my voice of reason. I'd cry on her bed and she'd comfort me. She'd tell me I was beautiful and smart. Michelle would let me stay with her as long as I wanted. I'd leave early for school and pick her up along the way, then stay late at her house after school and softball practice. Sometimes I'd have to sneak in and out so her parents wouldn't see me.

Eventually, I learned to ignore my mother's words. They held no value for me and I was determined more than ever to not become like her and leave this town.

I pulled into the unkempt parking lot trying unsuccessfully to avoid the potholes. Grass grew in the giant cracks on the sidewalk leading up to the door. The building itself was in decent condition, white stucco. It probably covered a broken brick façade.

The door didn't open when I pulled it. It must be locked. Duh. There was a small red button just to the left of the handle so I pushed it.

"County Jail. Who are you here to see?" The voice crackled and clicked.

"Um. Kim Teller. I'm her daughter. Jenna Mitchell."

"Pull the door when you hear the buzz." An atrociously loud buzz sounded. Birds fluttered away from the field across the way. A volcano probably erupted. I pulled open the door and walked in. There was another set of doors that was locked, but as soon as the door behind me shut, another buzzer sounded so I pulled on the second set of doors and it opened. There was a huge 1970's inspired reception desk in front of me. Dark wood paneling, a Formica top.

"Can I help you?" the bored receptionist inquired.

"Yes. I'm Jenna Mitchell. I'm here to see my mom, Kim Teller."

"Do you have an appointment?"

"Oh, no. I didn't know I needed one. My dad told me she wanted to see me, so I just drove over here."

"Hang on." She picked up the tan colored phone and relayed

the information I'd given her. She pushed the horn-rimmed glasses up on her nose while she waited for the information on the other end. Did we go back in time? Was this 1970?

"Have a seat," she said motioning toward the plastic chairs lining the adjacent wall.

I didn't wait long. A fat police officer waddled through a door I hadn't noticed before.

"Ms. Mitchell?"

"Yes."

"Follow me."

We walked down a long white hallway with doors and windows. I peered in some. People sat in high back chairs and stared at computer screens. Offices I guessed. We went through another set of doors that required us to stand uncomfortably close while we waited for them to unlock.

"This way." He motioned for me to follow him.

There wasn't any other way to go but straight. I followed him to the end of the hallway, then right into a room with old school desks and a few tables and chairs. Another police officer sat behind a huge metal teacher's desk. Only half the fluorescent lights were lit, casting a dim glow over the room.

"Have a seat. We'll bring your mom in."

Okay then. I sat at a small table with two chairs opposite each other. Last time I'd seen my mother she was on the other side of some Plexiglas and I'd spoken to her on a phone.

"Last time I had to talk to her through Plexiglas. I don't have to do that now?" I asked the officer at the desk.

"No. Her restrictions have changed since then. She can have supervised visits in a visitation room."

"Gotcha."

A million years passed before the fat officer returned to the suffocating room with my mother in tow. She was hidden behind him at first then he moved to the side and I was met with crazy. My mother looked crazy. She kind of always did, but she kept herself neat and presentable for the public. I mean, as presentable as a drug-dealing whore could look. Now, her normally sleek ringlet curls were a spirally, tangled mess. She was rail thin, and her skin was thin and pasty.

"Jenna. You came. You look fat," she croaked. Like really croaked. She sounded as awful as she looked.

I just sighed heavily. Not even thirty seconds in and she had already flung an insult at me.

She hobbled over to the table and sat in the chair across from me. A pang of sympathy passed over my heart as I watched her struggling to pull out the chair. My mother was in her early forties, but she looked as though she was pushing eighty. She didn't seem to be bothered by her own appearance though. She looked over at the desk officer and winked at him. I rolled my eyes.

"Well you look…" I couldn't be mean. Well I could, but the sight of her blocked my brain from thinking of anything else but how awful she looked.

"I look like shit Jenna, but at least I'm not fat." Good lord I had better make this visit quick.

"Okay then."

"Why are you back in town? There's nothing left for you here."

"I'm just back for summer break. I'm in college now Mom."

"Yeah, I heard that. Why?"

"So I can be better than you."

"You are a quippy one, aren't you?" She sat back in her chair and winked at the officer again.

I wondered if she was hoping I'd failed at whatever she'd thought I'd been doing for the last year and a half and wanted me to start up in the 'family business. Well, I had news for her: Not only was I not failing, I was thriving. I was at the top of my class at Brookhaven College, I was starting first base player for their softball team, and I had two great friendships there too. My life was far from failure, but it was hardly a success either.

Not that I could tell her any of that and she would care. She'd say I was showing off. I studied her for a minute. I had her eyes, hazel, but hers had more green in them. Now, they were faded to a dull brown and were sunken into her face, half hidden under her bushy eyebrows. While her hair was blonde and natural curly, I'd gotten my board straight, brown hair from my dad. I stared at her, but she barely looked at me. Her eyes flitted around the room looking at everything but me. She winked at the officer assigned to babysit us. He was tall and thin with dark hair and bright blue eyes. He reminded me of Andrew except for the eyes. He was sitting behind the old metal desk, leaning back in the office chair with his legs propped up on the desktop.

When she winked at him a second time, I slammed my hand on the table between us. I was not here to watch her flirt with her prison guards.

"Mom," I said loud enough to focus her attention back on me.

"What? He's cute. And young."

"Oh God, Mom. Is that all you think about?"

"Honey, I've got nothing better to do in here than to think about all the things I'd like to do to these fine young men." She winked at the officer again.

"You should do him. He's cute. You might be too fat though. No one likes a fat whore," she said and leaned back in her chair.

The officer grunted and shifted again.

"Mom. Stop. I came to see you because Dad told me to. There's a reason I haven't visited you since you were booked and you're displaying that reason now."

"Oh Jenna, unwind your panties. Take them off and air them out for a while."

I hung my head in embarrassment and shame.

"Are you living in the house?" she asked me quietly. I picked my head up and looked at her. She'd leaned close to me on the desk and hunched her shoulders.

"Yeah."

"Have you gone in my room?" she whispered.

"No," I said back in a normal voice.

She leaned in closer and wiggled her finger at me to do the same.

"Under my bed is…"

"I don't want to know." I knew exactly what she was going to tell me and I didn't want to know. "It's going in the trash!" I hissed at her.

"You will not. It's a grand's worth at least. Probably more

now."

"Trash. It's going in the trash and we're done." I stood to leave. The grunty officer stood too and moved around the desk.

"Jenna please. I'll get it out of the house, just don't get rid of it."

I didn't want to hear anymore. I don't know what I was expecting when I visited. I was fine with the insults, I'd learned to ignore those, but asking me to participate in her twisted life was unacceptable.

"I'm done. Take her back."

The fat officer met me at the door and we walked back down the sterile hallway. All kinds of scenarios raced through my mind. I didn't even want to think about drugs hiding in my house. I had to get rid of them before something bad happened. Would my mom make a phone call and tell on me? Surely I couldn't get in trouble for this. I didn't even know it was there. I hadn't even been in her room! I hated that I was sleeping in that house. Who knew what else was in there.

"Sorry about my mom." I said to him.

"It's okay that kind of thing happens all the time."

"Prisoners flirt with you all the time?"

"Yes." He laughed.

There was a shuffle at the end of the hall and we both turned to see what it was.

"Jenna!" my mom yelled from the end of the hall. "You are my daughter. Please…"

"No. No." I didn't even let her finish. I stalked off in the opposite direction leaving her and the tall officer behind me. I needed to get out of here quickly.

I burst through the front doors of the jailhouse completely ignoring the receptionist when she said bye to me. Even though the air outside was stiflingly hot, it was not as suffocating as the air inside. I took a few deep breaths before getting into my car.

The drugs were on my mind the entire way home. I slammed open the door to the house and stomped to her bedroom door. I stood there in front of it like an idiot. I couldn't make my hand open the door. My mind raced back to the times I'd be curled up in bed and I'd hear her escapades through the wall. I moved my bed to the opposite wall. It didn't really help. Eventually I bought an iPod with earphones and learned to sleep with music blasting through my brain.

Ugh. I forced my hand to turn the knob and push the door open. It swung wide knocking loose some cobwebs. Great, spiders. I loved spiders. Not really. I surveyed the room from the doorway. It was surprisingly clean. Dust had settled on everything. Her bed stood on a frame only, no head or footboard. The comforter was scrunched to the end of the bed. She'd probably been with someone before she went to the mayor's house and hurried them out. I knew that she and Michelle's dad were found at his house though, so it wasn't him.

The carpet was stained like it was in the rest of the house. I didn't even want to begin to think about what each stain could be. I'd have to touch the carpet if I wanted to see what was under the bed. No. I quickly ran to my room and searched for some gloves. I found some flimsy cotton winter gloves in my sock drawer. Good enough. I didn't want my fingerprints on whatever was under there anyway.

I returned to my mom's room and walked right in. The cigarette smell was strong in here. I hadn't aired it out like the rest of the house. I knelt down at the foot of the bed and looked under. I didn't see anything. I pulled out my phone and turned on the flashlight and shone it around the edge of the box spring.

Got it. Two small bags of white powder. I dumped them in the trash and took the trash to the curb. I still didn't know when trash day was but hopefully soon. I did not want that near my house any longer. I walked slowly back to the house. The day had exhausted me. I wasn't sure what I was expecting from the visit with my mom, but it was not discovering drugs were still in the house.

I hid in my room for the rest of the day. I closed my mother's door and crawled into bed. I grabbed a book but I doubted I'd read any of it. I didn't. I just flipped mindlessly through the pages. My phone buzzed, I looked at the caller ID. Andrew. Nope. Didn't really want to talk to him so I ignored it. I didn't feel like talking to anyone.

I tossed the book on the floor, rolled over in bed, and closed my eyes. Eventually I fell into a restless sleep.

CHAPTER SIX

I must have fallen asleep because I was rudely awoken by loud banging on my front door. I froze. I was still disoriented from sleep, but the paranoia of having an illegal substance in and around my house was still present. The fading sunlight told me it was late evening. Were the cops here? Did someone dig through my trash? The banging got louder and there was yelling. Shit. I stumbled out of bed, the paranoia made me shake so violently that I wasn't sure I'd make it to the front door. Whoever was there was just going to have to bust the door down. My phone buzzed on the bedside table. I grabbed it. Josh's name and number flashed across the screen. Oh thank God!

"Josh?!" I squeaked, the fear obvious in my voice.

"Jenna? Are you ok, I'm at the door?"

I breathed a massive sigh of relief. I regained my composure and walked to the front door and opened it for him.

"Are you ok? I've been calling for a couple hours," he said, shoving his phone in his back pocket. I did the same.

"I'm fine. I visited my mom then I fell asleep." There was no way I was telling him there were drugs in my trash can.

"You visited your mom? Why?"

"My dad asked me to. I guess she called him."

"Your Dad?"

"Yeah. Usually it requires a mom and a dad to make a baby." His questions were annoying me in my half-sleepy, half panicked state.

"I just meant that I didn't know you had contact with him."

"I do. He's paid the bills on this house my entire life. I went to live with him when my mom went to jail. He lives about five hours south of here in Brookhaven."

"I see," he said in a noncommittal sort of way.

"Why are you here Josh?" I asked. I was still tired and I just wanted to go back to bed. Today had been long enough.

"Well I called and you didn't answer. I was worried."

"Why? There's not much for me to do to get into trouble around here." As soon as I said that I knew what he was thinking. There was plenty I could do. Today's events proved that.

"I just worry about you alone in this house," he said. He sheepishly ran his fingers through his hair. I replayed that action in my head a few times and thought how nice it would be if I could run my fingers through his hair. Or if he would run his fingers through my hair.

"Jenna." Josh was right in my face.

"Sorry." Now I was the sheepish one. "I'm fine. Nothing to be worried about, I was just sleeping."

Josh looked me up and down. I probably looked like crap. I ran my hands through my hair and realized the ponytail I'd had it in was lopsided and hair was falling out of it. I rolled my eyes in embarrassment. At least I was wearing clothes. I hadn't meant to fall asleep earlier so I was still wearing the clothes I'd gone to the jail in.

"What are you doing now?" he asked. He was still standing outside on the porch, I hadn't invited him in.

"Uh, well, I was sleeping," I trailed off.

I didn't even know what time it was. I'd gone to the jail around ten and judging by the light outside I'd have to guess is was late afternoon or early evening.

"Right." He looked down at his dirty work boots.

"Are you hungry? I could make lunch, or dinner, whatever time it is." I moved out of the way and let Josh in.

"Dinner sounds good, its 5:15," he said excitedly. "Do you have more than peanut butter and jelly?" He nudged me aside when we walked into the house.

I closed the front door and followed him into my kitchen. I'd braved a trip to Miller's the day after our date. I hadn't run into anyone, thank God, but I was able to pick up some basics besides sandwich fixings.

"Yes, I do. I went down to the store the other day and grabbed a frozen lasagna."

"Sounds delicious."

It didn't take long to prepare the lasagna. Preheat the oven, insert lasagna, cook for an hour, enjoy. After I'd put it in the oven, Josh and I walked into the living room and sunk into the ugly couch.

"Do you have cable?" he asked and reached for the remote.

"Not yet. Hopefully next week."

His face fell. Maybe he had changed his mind about staying for dinner.

"So what do you want to do?" he asked. Nope. He was determined to stay.

Make out. No, I didn't really say that. I surely thought about it though. I was all talk and no action sometimes.

"Umm…"

"What do you usually do in the evenings?"

"Read."

"Oh."

"What do you usually do?" I asked.

"Watch TV or play video games."

"I see."

We sat in uncomfortable silence for a bit.

"I could read to you." That sounded super dumb coming out of my mouth.

"No, that's okay. When are you going to get your TV hooked up again?

"Sometime next week." I was a little bummed about him not wanting me to read to him. It would be a way for us to hang out together privately.

"Well we could watch movies together. I have a ton of them."

"Yeah I have some too." I tried to hide the disappointment in my voice. I didn't watch much TV, but if it meant spending time with Josh, then I'd watch anything.

"Or I could teach you how to play video games."

"Let's just stick to movies for now."

"Okay."

"I could even cook for you."

It sounded to me like we were making plans for multiple nights of movie watching.

"You mean reheat already cooked frozen dinners?" Josh made

fun of me.

"Don't diss my culinary skills!" I punched him lightly in the arm.

"Ow! Okay okay!" He pretended to be hurt.

"I just realized I don't have a VCR or DVD player."

"Well that makes it hard to watch a movie."

"I have my laptop!" I jumped up off the couch.

"That'll work."

I ran to my bedroom and grabbed my laptop bag. When I returned I set up the computer on the coffee table.

"What movie do you want to watch?"

"What do you have?"

"Probably just a bunch of Disney movies."

"Hmmm…I'm not really sure I've seen many Disney movies."

"Are you serious?!" I faced him, wide eyed.

"Yeah." He rubbed the back of his neck.

"You didn't watch them as a child?"

"My grandmother thinks Disney is from the devil."

"Your grandmother is kind of crazy."

"Yeah."

I scanned the DVD titles in the small TV cabinet and just grabbed one at random. I flipped the case so he could see it and I could tell he wasn't interested by the way he scrunched up his nose.

"The Little Mermaid? Really?"

"You knocked my reading idea and left me to choose the activity." I teased.

"Fine, but tomorrow it's my turn to pick."

"Deal."

I felt the stress of the day leave my body as Josh and I settled a little further into the couch. The movie started. It took all I had to not sing along with every song. I'd forgotten how much I loved this movie. I used to have a TV in my room when I was younger and I'd watch this movie on repeat just to drown out the noise that came from my mother's room.

Halfway through the movie, the oven timer went off.

"Your dinner is ready," I said over the obnoxious beeping.

After we ate, we finished watching the movie and I started washing the dishes in the sink. Josh lingered in the kitchen and leaned against the counter to watch me. There wasn't much to wash, just the dishes from tonight and what little I'd used over the last couple days. I washed, he dried. I was getting tired though and I really wanted to go to sleep. The events of earlier in the day still weighed heavily on my mind and my body was still tense from being paranoid. I still was. The trashcan was still out there. When was trash day?

"Um, I should get to bed," I said when we'd finished.

"Yeah. I should go. I'll see you tomorrow though, right?"

"Yes, of course. I want to know what your pick is for movie night."

We both laughed.

Josh and I lingered at the door, neither too sure how to end the night. Our non-kiss at the end of our date seemed to hamper both of us tonight. I wanted him to kiss me but I also didn't want to seem too eager. Why was this so difficult? We'd been friends for years, heck, we'd even dated and kissed before, why was this any different?

Eventually, Josh turned to leave. I waved at his back as he turned in the doorway and brushed his arm when I let my arm fall. He turned his head back to me and smiled before descending the steps, skipping the second one, because he remembered that it was faulty.

I really was exhausted, but I showered quickly and climbed into bed naked and wet. My thoughts immediately turned to Josh. Our date last week was nice, but tonight was how I remembered us, easy conversations, and a little playfulness. It was starting to feel like it used to be between us, back when we were just friends; back when we were us.

CHAPTER SEVEN

I called Dad to tell him about the visit with Mom. I conveniently left out the part about the drugs in my house. I'm sure he wouldn't let me stay if he knew about that. We talked for a few minutes longer and he mentioned that he, Linda, and the kids were leaving for vacation in Florida next week and would be gone for two weeks, then the kids went to camp, and he and Linda were off to Mexico for a while. Of course I was jealous. I'd never been to Florida or Mexico, or any kind of vacation.

Josh and I spent the next two weeks watching all of the Disney movies I owned and countless car movies Josh had brought over, plus some random shows on cable after it had been hooked up. We had settled into a strange routine. He'd come over after work and we'd watch a movie and eat dinner then we washed the dishes together. I actually rather hated it. I felt like we were in seventh grade and neither of us knew how to act around the opposite sex. We would sit really close to each other on the couch, or he would lay with his head in my lap, or sometimes he'd hold my feet in his lap and rub them. It was weird the first time he did that, but now it was almost normal. And while I liked our closeness and him touching me, I wanted more. We weren't in seventh grade anymore, we were adults (practically), and we could touch each other in an adult way.

We talked sometimes, but not about anything important. He explained exactly what he did on the farm and how his school would help him in the future. I talked to him about my plans to become a school guidance counselor because I wanted to help kids that were in similar situations as mine and encourage them that there was a life outside of this crappy life they'd been given. The one thing we didn't talk about was Michelle. I assumed they weren't dating anymore, but I wasn't for sure. I mean, he'd spent every night for the last two weeks at my house, so obviously they weren't together, but I still felt weird because he didn't want to talk about her, and she was nowhere to be found so I could talk to her myself. I wasn't a man stealer, but if he was choosing me over her, I wasn't going to complain.

So tonight, I decided to try a little harder to snag him. I dressed myself in black leggings and a long grey cardigan sweater with owls stitched on the sleeves over a white lace trimmed camisole over a red bra. Yeah, I was going there. It was comfy, a little sexy, and way better than the jeans and old t-shirts I had been wearing. I'd even curled my long hair and left it down. Ponytails were for ten year olds. The doorbell rang while I was still primping in the bathroom. I slathered on some lip gloss and hurried to answer the door.

"Hey," I said a little breathless. The house wasn't that big, but the sight of him tonight took the words right out of my mouth. It looks like he'd had the same idea. He was dressed in dark denim jeans and white button down shirt. He'd also traded his usual brown steel-toed work boots for leather cowboy boots.

"Well hey there gorgeous."

I blushed. "Hey yourself."

"Can I come in?"

"Yes!" I said a little too excitedly and moved out of the doorway.

"What are we watching tonight?" he asked.

"Yeah. Lasagna's in the oven," I said first. "And I pick Harry Potter. It should last us a week."

He just laughed and sat on the couch. It was my turn for a movie and I'd chosen Harry Potter. Last night he'd said he was out of ideas and DVD's so I should choose what to watch for the next week. Eight Harry Potter movies seemed like the perfect fit. I popped the movie in, grabbed the remotes, and joined him on the couch. Josh scooted close to me and wrapped his arm around my back and pulled me close to him.

Somehow over the next forty-five minutes we'd intertwined ourselves up in each other. My legs were on his and his arms were around me. When the oven timer went off I untangled myself from him and rushed to the kitchen to turn it off and pull out the lasagna.

"I'm not really hungry." Josh said as he wandered into the kitchen.

I decided to cover it up and put it in the fridge. Back in the living room he sat back down next to me. I shifted so that I was leaning against the arm of the couch and slung my legs up and laid them Josh's lap. He only smiled as I settled in to finish the movie.

As we watched the movie, Josh traced slow circles over my feet and ankles that sent tingles up between my legs. If he kept doing that I wasn't sure how much longer I was going to be able to concentrate on the movie before I jumped into his lap. His wildly intoxicating cologne filled my senses with hints of citrus and wood and something warm that filtered down, meeting the tingles sent from his fingers at my feet. Shivers passed over me and deep through my body, the combination of his scent and his hands on me took me over the edge. I pulled my feet back and leaned close to him.

"I can't concentrate with you rubbing my feet like that," I said softly.

He let out a quick chuckle like he knew what he was doing to me. He just stared at me for an uncomfortable amount of time. He did know what he was doing to me.

"Because you need to concentrate really hard on a movie you've probably seen a hundred times?" he mumbled.

"What?" I said.

"Nothing," he said, but smiled at me.

"Why are you staring at me?"

"I'm not allowed to look at you?"

"You can look at me, but you're staring and it's weirding me out."

"Weirding you out?"

"Yeah." My voice was getting smaller and smaller each time he asked me a question.

"I just like looking at you. You're beautiful."

"Are you drunk?" I asked.

"No, I think you're beautiful."

"Stop."

"Stop what?"

"You shouldn't say things like that."

"What things?"

"Things like that!" Now I was getting annoyed. What was he playing at?

"Well then what can I do?"

"I don't know!"

We sat there staring at each other. Neither of us moved. A sly smile crept across Josh's face and I couldn't help but smile as well.

"What?" he asked.

"You smiled first!" I responded.

"So? I like smiling."

"Smiling's my favorite."

"Oh good, you know that movie. I was afraid we'd have to stop being friends."

I laughed. Elf was one of my favorite Christmas movies. I could quote pretty much the entire movie.

Josh suddenly leaned really close to me. His face was in my personal bubble, but I didn't care. I liked it there.

This was what I had been waiting for. I'm not sure why I was waiting for him to make the move, but here we were. Moves were being made, obviously I wanted more as well, but Michelle always popped in my head. She and Josh had been dating when the fiasco with her dad and my mom happened, but she wasn't here now. Who knew where she was. Josh did. But at this moment I didn't care. She wasn't here to claim him, so I would. Josh's warm breath on my face reminded me of our proximity to each other. You know what Michelle? Screw you. You can't even pick up your phone to call to say hi, and your boyfriend has been at my house every day for the past two weeks so obviously you aren't dating anymore. He's mine now.

Bitchy move, but at this moment I really didn't care. At all.

I closed the short distance between us and placed my lips hesitantly against his. I wanted him to respond to my kiss. To press his lips into mine. I waited but got nothing more than a small pucker so I pulled away.

"Um," I managed.

"Yeah."

"I just wanted to kiss you," I said breathlessly.

"I wanted you to kiss me," he replied. Then why didn't he kiss me back? Was he thinking about Michelle too? God I hoped not.

We sat like this for a few more seconds, just staring, inches from each other. He suddenly pulled me to him, positioning each of my legs alongside his so I was straddling him. He looked up at me and I looked down at him. His hands were on my hips and held me firmly against him. Our prolonged closeness was only fueling the desire that welled up inside me. I grasped his face and pulled him into a hard, teeth-knocking kiss. This time he kissed me back. Our mouths melded together, our tongues swirling around each other's. I rocked my hips against his sending him into a flurry of hands finding their way under my shirt. His cold hands against the warm skin of my back made me gasp and arch against him. We parted and he looked down at my chest that was just inches from his face. I smiled at his expression. He almost looked hungry.

Josh looked back up at me and smiled. He pressed his hands against my lower back causing me to fall forward into him. I braced myself against the back of the couch and continued to rock against him, his face in my chest.

"Jenna?" Josh breathed.

"Yes," I whispered back.

He responded back with a slow kiss that told me we were stopping. I gripped his face in my hands and held on to the kiss for a beat longer, then let him go.

"That was amazing," he said finally, I wasn't sure if I should move or stay. His hands were still pressing against my back so it was arched against his chest.

"I'm glad you thought so."

"Can I take you out again? There's something I want to show you."

This was random.

"Yeah sure. But can we just stay closer. I don't need to go to the city."

"Okay. Well that just makes it easier. How about next week sometime?"

"Yeah. Okay." I couldn't help but smile at him. "Can I kiss you again?"

"Yes."

His lips were soft against mine this time as he slowly caressed my mouth. His hands left my back, traveled down my thighs, then back up and settled on my hips.

I wanted Josh to stay the night. I knew he was thinking about it too.

"Josh," I whispered between kisses.

"The movie's over," he whispered back.

I didn't say anything, I just pulled back away from him and looked him in the eyes. I tried to keep a straight face, but I couldn't and cracked a smile, then laughed out loud.

"What's so funny?" he asked.

"I don't know. You, us, this whole situation."

"What about it?" he asked.

Josh shifted underneath me so I toppled forward, hovering over his face, my arms braced against the arm of the couch. He grinned up at me and stared down at my lips, then lower down my shirt.

"I just wasn't expecting this, us," I whispered.

"What about us?" he asked. He reached up and brushed my lips softly. Electric shocks raced through my lips and my whole body. I took a deep breath and looked him in the eyes.

"I don't know. I just wanted to have a quiet summer, clean up the house so my dad could sell it, and leave. Just kind of bring closure to this part of my life. I'll probably never come back here again."

"And you thought you could find closure without seeing me?" He sounded serious, but he was still smiling.

"Well, yeah. I don't know. I had a plan in my head and you ruined it the first day I got here."

"How did I do that?" he asked.

"In the grocery store. I know we didn't have much or date much before I left, but we were friends, and I felt safe with you."

Josh didn't respond right away. His eyes were searching my face, like he was looking for me to tell him what to say. He shifted again and sat up on the couch. He leaned against the arm of the couch. I slid down so I was resting on his thighs.

"Jenna. You and I were best friends. We always have been.

When we were dating," he paused, his face scrunched like he was trying to find the right words, "it felt right, and wrong all at the same time. Like, you were the right person, but it was the wrong time, and then my mom just didn't like you." He added the last part quickly.

I knew why his mom didn't like me, but I didn't want to bring that up in case he didn't know my mom had slept with his dad. I sighed happily though because I felt like I was being given a second chance with Josh. Even if it was just for the summer. Maybe I needed more closure than I thought.

"Okay," was all I said before I leaned in and kissed him. He grasped the back of my neck and kissed me back. His tongue slipped in and out of my mouth. I leaned forward more so I was resting on his hips again and I wrapped my arms around his neck. He raised his hips against mine, I didn't know if he was shifting again or if it was an intentional move. Desire flooded through me and I pressed myself closer to him. He kissed me harder now and threaded his fingers through my hair. He lifted his hips again. I rocked against him in response.

Josh broke our kiss and looked deep into my eyes. We were both breathing heavily at this point. I wanted him and I knew he wanted me.

"Not right now Jenna," he said.

"Why not?" I kissed him again.

"Because I don't want it to happen on an ugly couch," he laughed.

I swatted at his chest but he caught me by my wrists and held them just above him.

"Okay. Well then you should probably go, unless you want to move this to my bedroom."

Josh looked up and behind him toward the direction of my room. He was contemplating my suggestion.

"I should probably go. It's getting late and I do have to work tomorrow." He sighed again and made a move to get up.

I climbed off of him and straightened my clothing, he did the same. I walked him the short distance to the front door and opened it for him. Before he left, he turned to face me and pinned me against the wall.

"I'm here for you Jenna. I'm not going anywhere and I'm not letting other people get in our way this time. It's you and me." He kissed me again then left.

I pondered his last comment. He wasn't going to go anywhere, but I wasn't staying here. Did he think I would? I had school to finish five hours away. Did he want me to come back when I was done? I thought about Andrew. I should call him. Even though we weren't exclusively together, I felt like what I was doing with Josh was somehow cheating. And I'd been ignoring his calls since I'd been here.

I walked back to my bedroom and flopped down on the bed, still in my clothes. I stared at the ceiling and tried to sort out what was happening with Josh.

CHAPTER EIGHT

The next morning I was awoken by banging on my front door. Good grief, I had a doorbell. I bet it was Josh again. I smiled to myself. I missed him already and I could use a kiss. He'd left me wanting so much more when he left last night. I had laid in bed for an hour just thinking about the two of us before I'd fallen asleep. I wanted to talk to him about what his expectations were about us and tell him that I wasn't sure I wanted to be in Riverview after this summer.

The pounding on my door continued at steady pace, almost rhythmic. Who the hell was at my door? I'd fallen asleep in my clothes from last night so I quickly grabbed a hair tie and looped it through my hair into a low ponytail and made my way to the front door. *Maybe I should get Josh a key so he could just check on me whenever he wanted*, I thought to myself. It was a silly thought, but he'd been at my house every night for the past two weeks so it wasn't really that silly.

I stopped short when I saw a strange man leaning against the door. His head was resting on his raised forearm and the other hand was pounding relentlessly against the glass of the screen door. He wore a business suit with a red tie that was loosened around his collar.

The stranger straightened himself when he saw me. He wore a weary smile and was sweating already. I checked my phone, 10:00 am. It was probably already at least ninety degrees out. I opened the oak door, but left the screen door shut.

"Hi." I said.

"Jenna. Uh. I'm selling vacuums."

"What?"

"I'm selling vacuums. Do you want one?"

This guy was sweating pretty profusely and fidgeting with the collar of his of his shirt. Something told me that he did not sell vacuums.

"How did you know my name?" I asked.

"Your mom sent me."

"My mom?" I said more to myself than to him.

Who the heck was this guy and how did he know my mom? How did he know where I lived? "My mom is in jail."

This man began to shake and look back and forth to the street and back to me. He loosened his tie some more and unbuttoned the top button of his shirt. He took a step forward and reached for the handle of the screen door. I realized in that moment that I hadn't locked that door. He swung it open and stepped inside. He was taller than me, but rail thin. I could take him if I needed to.

"Listen little girl, your mother has something of mine and I'm here to get it. She said you would let me in." He'd taken off his blazer and tossed it on the couch. Did he think he was staying a while?

Crap. Realization smacked me in the face. He was here for the drugs! Did she call him from jail? I quickly looked past him and saw that the trash was gone. Of course it was gone, it had been two weeks since I'd seen my mother, and the trash had come and gone a few times since then.

"Um. I don't think there's anything here for you."

"Oh, there better be." He wheezed and spit the sweat that dripped from his face. I was completely disgusted and just wanted him out of my house.

Maybe there was more I didn't know about? I was probably making a bad decision letting him go look, but did I have a choice? I backed away from him and let him pass me. He surveyed the house like he'd been here before. He probably had. I never paid attention to the men who filtered through my mother's bedroom. I either locked myself in my room or went to Michelle's.

"Oh, okay."

At my word, he pushed past me and headed straight back to her room. There was no question now that he'd been here before.

"Hey!" I yelled. I wanted to go see what he was doing, but I was not interested in being any closer to him that necessary.

I heard some rustling of papers and the mattress fall. He came barreling out of the back rooms and into the living room. He got real close to me. Beads of sweat rained down his face.

"Where are they Jenna?" His voice was loud and panicked. "She told me they were here. Two bags." He raised two fingers up like a peace sign and pushed them into my face.

"I don't know what you're talking about." There was no way I was telling him I threw out potentially a grand worth of drugs.

"They were in her room, under her mattress. He told me they were there." He moved closer to me and put his hands on my shoulders and shook me. His eyes were wild now.

"He?"

The man looked confused for a split second, then remembered himself "She, whatever. Where are the bags?"

"I don't know." I found it odd that he had said 'he' instead of 'she'.

Suddenly the man threw me on the couch and followed me pushing, me into the thick cushions. He leaned his knee between my legs and pinned my shoulders with his hands.

"You are a lying little slut Jenna, just like your mom. Now I'll give you one more chance to tell me where they are." His voice was calm and quiet but his face was red with rage, his eyes bulged.

"Not here." My voice was calm, but I was scared shitless.

"Then where?" He growled and pressed into me.

"I don't know."

"You little liar!" He roared. He pulled at my camisole but I refused to let him touch me.

"Stop! Stop please!" I screamed.

"Tell me where they are and I will." His face had changed. His eyes were hungry.

I kicked my legs wildly, trying to hit any part of him that would make him stop. I stilled briefly to gather my strength, then burst my arms and legs outward and threw him off me. I thanked God I wasn't a petite girl.

He tumbled off the couch. I didn't wait around to tell him to get out of my house. I ran out the door, grabbed my discarded sweater from last night, and headed down the street. I knew where I would go and prayed he'd be home.

A car pulled up beside me making me jump to the side. I quickened my pace, I didn't want to explain to anyone why I was walking barefoot down the street at ten in the morning.

"Jenna!" A female voice called my name. It was Lauren in her cherry red Grand Am. She'd had that car in high school. I remembered being jealous of it. "What are you doing?"

"Walking," I replied. I didn't look at her, I was afraid she'd start asking too many questions.

"Do you want a ride?"

"That's okay. I'm just going to walk." I kept walking.

"Don't be silly. It's burning up already and the pavement has to be hot on your feet."

She was right, my bare feet were on fire. I stopped walking and contemplated what to do next. I just wanted to get to Josh's house. I'd only have to be in the car with her for a few minutes.

"Okay," I said and walked around the front of her car and got in.

"Where are we going?" Lauren asked.

"To Josh Riley's house."

"Alrighty."

"Thanks."

"Where are your shoes?"

"I forgot them."

"You forgot to put on shoes when you left the house?" she asked like I was the stupidest person alive. I probably was.

"Yes."

We rode in silence the rest of the way to Josh's house which really was only about a minute longer.

"Jenna," Lauren said before I could get out of the car.

"Yes," I was beyond annoyed.

"I don't know what's going on right now, but I wanted to let you know that I'm here for you, okay?"

Her sentiment stopped me from leaving. We both knew we weren't the best of friends, but she was reaching out to me now and I could tell she was being sincere.

"Thanks Lauren."

With that, I got out of the car and padded up the walkway to Josh's house. I paused before knocking on the door. Didn't Josh work all day? Crap. I didn't see his truck in the driveway. He probably wasn't even here. I pulled out my phone and dialed his number. It rang several times and I almost hung up.

"Hello?" He sounded distracted.

"Hey Josh," I said. I didn't mean for my voice to come out sounding so pathetic, but I was so shaken by what had just happened and I was out of breath from running here.

"Jen, what's wrong?" I knew had his full attention. I hoped he wasn't on a tractor or doing something potentially dangerous at the moment. His full attention was on me.

"Um. I'm at your house. Something happened."

"What happened?" His voice was escalating.

"I'd rather not discuss it over the phone. When will you be home?"

"Jenna, are you okay? I can be there in like twenty minutes. My mom should be there, knock on the door."

"Yeah. Okay. I'm okay," I said quickly.

I did as he instructed. A few seconds later, the door opened, revealing a tall slender woman with medium length brown hair and kind eyes stood in front of me. I'd always liked Josh's mom. She was like the town mom. She always made pie and random kids were always in and out of her house. Probably not so much anymore now that Josh was grown, but I had fond memories here as a child. I'm sure she liked me too until she found out my mother had slept with her husband. I was fifteen or sixteen when it happened. I didn't remember the details, but I remember Josh telling me that his dad was leaving.

"Hi, Mrs. Riley."

"Jenna?" I must have looked worse than I thought. "Can I help you?"

"Jenna, give your phone to my mom."

"Josh wants to talk to you," I said as I handed her my phone.

Mrs. Riley looked puzzled, but took my phone and spoke into it to Josh.

I looked away from her and tried not to eavesdrop. I straightened my cardigan and retied my hair. I was grateful I'd fallen asleep with my bra on last night otherwise showing up at Josh's house barefoot and half naked would have been extremely awkward.

'Hi Josh... Oh…Okay…Are you sure...If you think that's best sweetie…Okay…Love you too…Bye now." Mrs. Riley handed the phone back to me.

"Hey," I said taking the phone back. Their conversation was vague and confusing.

"I'll be there shortly," he said quickly.

"Okay. Bye."

I turned to Mrs. Riley. She looked me up and down again.

"Um. I'm sorry. I didn't know where else to go."

"It's okay. Come on in." She moved aside and let me in the house. "What happened sweetheart?"

She motioned for me to follow her to the kitchen. I wondered if she had a pie.

"Can we wait until Josh gets here?" I asked.

I didn't know what I even wanted to tell them. Did I tell them that I'd secretly, unbeknownst to me, had thousands of dollars' worth of drugs in my house and that my mother sent some random guy to get it, and that when I wouldn't tell him where they were he attacked me.

I looked around me while Mrs. Riley flitted around her kitchen pulling ingredients from several cabinets. The house was exactly as I remembered it. Light blue carpet covered the floors. There was wallpaper on every wall, some was peeling, and some was probably stuck there for life. It wasn't a dilapidated house by any means, but showed signs of disrepair. Signs that a struggling single mother lived here and did her best, but let a few things go in the process. Josh's dad was gone a lot when he was a kid, as a truck driver usually is.

In the kitchen, there was more wallpaper. It was bright yellow with small lighter yellow flowers with green centers. It wrapped around the top half of the walls, then artificial wood paneling continued at the bottom half. There was an island in the middle with a white Formica top. Two stools sat, tucked under the overhang. Mrs. Riley was gathering her ingredients there. It looked like pancakes. Pancakes would be amazing. I'd stocked up on sugary fruity cereal the last time I went to Miller's. I usually tried to eat healthy, but I was on my own and the white bunny was staring at me from the box, pleading with me to buy his cereal. Not that pancakes would be less sugary but they would taste way better. I sat in silence and watched her prepare whatever she was preparing.

"I hope you like pancakes," she finally said.

"I do. Thank you."

"Are you and Josh together?" she asked.

"Uh. I don't know."

I watched as she added the flour, sugar, and baking powder to a bowl and whisked them all together.

"Well he's been over at your house every night for the last few weeks now."

I laughed nervously and looked down at my hands on the table. "Yeah, we've been watching Disney princess movies.

"You expect me to believe that the two of you are in a house alone together and all you do is watch cartoons?"

"Well sometimes we watch movies that Josh likes," I countered.

"I see." She plopped two eggs into the bowl of flour along with some milk and mixed the ingredients until they were smooth.

"You can believe what you want, but that's what we do. I cook him dinner too." My phone chose that moment to start ringing. I grabbed it quickly and silenced it but not before I saw who it was. Andrew. I really should answer it.

"Boyfriend back home?" she asked. I didn't respond.

"I'm not here to cause trouble, Mrs. Riley."

"Then why are you here, Jenna? Why did you come back?" She didn't sound like she was accusing me of anything but I couldn't help but feel like she was.

"I'm just here for the summer, to clean out the house because my dad wants to sell it. I'm in school full time. I just didn't want to live with my dad and his wife this summer."

"I see. I can imagine how awkward that might be." She turned back to her cooking.

Where was Josh? It seemed as though his mom wasn't happy to see me here. Here in town or here at her house. I contemplated just leaving, but I didn't know if that man was still at my house, or if I'd meet him along the way. Besides, I really wanted pancakes.

Josh burst through the door at that moment and I was pulled from my thoughts. His dark denim jeans were covered in mud to the point where I could barely tell they were blue. The mud also covered the bottom of his plain white shirt. Splatters covered his arms, neck, and face as well. There was even mud clinging to his sun bleached blond hair.

I knew I was staring, but I couldn't help myself.

"Josh! Don't come in here like that!" I glanced quickly out of the corner of my eye at Mrs. Riley. She rushed over to him and pushed him toward a door just to the right of the back door.

"Then what am I supposed to do? I need to change and shower," Josh said. He sounded annoyed.

"Go to the laundry room." She ushered him to a door off the side of the kitchen. "Take off your clothes in there and grab a towel and go to the bathroom. What happened?"

"Cows were stubborn."

Josh pulled off his shirt before he disappeared into the laundry room. His back and shoulder muscles rippled under his tanned skin. I followed the line of his back all the way down to the waistband of his jeans. Mud covered the lower half of his torso.

Mrs. Riley continued with the pancake making while Josh rustled around in the laundry room. I couldn't help but let my mind slip into a daydream. Me, Josh, mud. You get the picture.

"Jenna," Mrs. Riley said sharply, "come help me finish up these pancakes." I snapped out of my drool-inducing daydream.

I wandered over to her and smiled stupidly when she handed me a spatula. I sucked at flipping pancakes. Not that I had much practice. In the dorms at school, one of my roommates had an electric griddle so we made pancakes sometimes. I never was able to get the cake to turn over without glopping the batter all over. Either that or I'd burn one side so they never were perfect. Josh's mom on the other hand was perfect. She poured out the batter in perfectly even, round circles. She flipped with perfection too. No batter glopping.

"You make perfect pancakes," I said.

"Well thank you, dear."

We worked in silence. She poured the batter and flipped, I took the cakes off the griddle and stacked them on the platter.

"Jenna. I hope you'll forgive me for my attitude earlier. I wasn't trying to be rude."

"Of course," I knew what she was talking about.

"It's just that with your mother's reputation you can understand why I was concerned."

"Mrs. Riley," I said turned to face her, "I really like Josh and I would never intentionally hurt him. He's the only person who even talks to me in this town. Well, besides Lauren, but only when she has to at the store. Michelle hasn't even called, I'm not sure she even knows I'm here. I want to go see her, but now I'm not so sure."

"Mom!" Josh's voice barked from behind us, making us both jump.

I turned to look at him. He was dressed in clean blue jeans and a new white t-shirt. His hair was still damp and tiny droplets trickled down the side of his face.

"Josh!" Mrs. Riley exclaimed, "I didn't even hear you go to the shower. And I didn't say anything."

"Jenna, what happened?" Josh said changing the subject before I could ask anything else.

Mrs. Riley nodded at me and I'm relieved from my spatula duty. I sat at the table with Josh. The water still in his hair reflected the early afternoon sun that streamed through the window. He smelled divine, like a Christmas tree farm or something. Good. Really good.

"Um. A man dressed in a suit came to my house this morning."

"Okay," Josh said calmly from across the table.

"He said he was selling vacuums, I didn't believe him, then he said my mom sent him and he pushed his way into the house and searched it for drugs.

"What?" Josh yelled and stood up. "Did he hurt you?" His eyes searched my face, then the rest of my body that he could see.

"He pushed me onto the couch, but I pushed him off me and

ran here."

"How did your mom contact him?" Mrs. Riley asked when she set the pancakes on the table. She then opened the refrigerator and pulled out maple syrup and butter.

"I don't know," I said.

"How does your mom even know you are here?" Mrs. Riley asked.

"Um. I visited her a couple weeks ago." I paused. I still wasn't sure I wanted to tell either of them about the drugs, but I did anyway. "She told me she still had drugs hidden in the house." Tears welled up in my eyes.

"We have to call the police," Mrs. Riley said.

"There's more. I didn't want them in my house so I threw them in the trash the day I saw her."

"So the guy was there for the drugs?" Josh asked.

"He came over looking for them. He forced his way into the house, ransacked my mother's room, and then pushed me around a little before he realized I wasn't going to tell him where they were. I pushed him off me and ran out of my house. I don't know if he's still there or what." I repeated the information again for him.

"Oh my goodness! You poor child." Mrs. Riley pulled me into a side hug, wrapping her arms protectively around my head and shoulders.

"I don't know what to do! I'm not here for trouble. I really just came back to have a quiet summer." I was crying now. Hot tears streamed down my face as I remembered the man's hands on me. I decided to leave the part out about him trying to rip off my shirt.

"Oh honey. It's okay. I still think we should call the police. Maybe they can search your house for anything else. Did he tell you his name?"

"No. But he was tall with short dark hair and eyes. He had on a red tie. There were two baggies in my mom's room. I hadn't even gone in there until that day. I had no idea."

"I know. I believe you," she said quietly.

"You do?" I looked up at her. Her expression was sincere.

"Josh honey, why don't you drive Jenna back to her house and see if he's still there? I'll call the police and meet you up there."

"I don't want to cause trouble."

"I'll tell them someone broke in. You were here eating breakfast this morning when it happened."

Mrs. Riley was lying for me. I smiled at her then followed Josh out to his truck. He'd been silent through the entire exchange. The drive back up to my house was silent too. I wanted to say something but I wasn't sure what.

My front door was open when we pulled up. The house was a disaster. He'd removed all the cushions from my ugly couch and flipped it. The end table was turned over. All the kitchen cabinets were open as well as the ones in the bathroom. My room was completely taken apart and my clothes had been thrown out of the closet. It looked like he'd taken a second pass at my mother's room as well. Josh had gone in first to make sure it was all clear and I found him back in the living room, putting the couch back together so we could sit on it.

"Here," he said, and handing me my necklace. "I found it on the floor."

I touched my neck. I hadn't even noticed. I took it from him and tried to reclasp it, but it was broken.

"It's broken."

The crunching of the gravel announced the arrival of the police and Mrs. Riley. I let them in and retold the same story I'd told Josh and his mom in their kitchen. We left out the fact that I was home at the time They told me that if I came across any more drugs that I should call them immediately. I agreed and they left after taking some pictures and going over my statement again.

"I don't want you here alone anymore." Josh said.

"I don't have anywhere else to go. I can't go back to school yet, and my dad and Linda are in Florida with their kids on vacation."

"And you didn't go with them?" Mrs. Riley asked.

"Linda doesn't like me. You can imagine why."

"You can stay with us." Josh said.

Mrs. Riley and I looked at each other. Neither of us wanted that. I understand both of their concern, but me living with Josh and his mom was just not an option.

"No. I couldn't impose on you."

"Then I'll stay here. I'll sleep on the couch."

"Oh Josh, honey. That's not necessary," his mom said.

"Yes it is. She can't be here alone!"

"I'll be fine. You're here every evening anyway. Seriously. I don't want you to stay here."

Josh wasn't happy. I was kicking myself for declining his offer. I would feel safer and lord knows I wanted Josh in my bed, but I didn't need more gossip. This "robbery" was already going to be the talk of the town if it got out. I didn't need Josh caught up in the mix. I wondered if Michelle would call me now.

Josh and his mom stayed for a little while longer to help me clean up and straighten the house. Once again, I ignored my mother's room. I just closed the door and pretended it wasn't even there. Once everything was back in order, Mrs. Riley left.

"You won't be alone in this house anymore. I will stay here if I have to."

"What about your mom?"

"I don't care. It's not safe. What if he comes back?"

"I don't know. He could have broken in the first time but he knocked."

"But he attacked you."

"I know! I know," I said a little quieter. "I'm scared. I don't even know how he knew to come. My mom must have called him but I didn't know prisoners could just call whoever they wanted."

"Maybe you should call her and ask. You never know who else she might have called or who else could stop by."

That thought was terrifying. How many people could she contact? Would more crazed men come pounding at my door looking for drugs or worse? This whole situation was becoming more horrible by the second. What was I supposed to do now?

"No, I just want to be done with my mom. I didn't come back to see her. I did. Now I'm done."

"Well you're not done if she's going to send random men to your house."

Josh had a point. Why was this happening to me? I wanted to scream that out to the sky. Not that anyone would hear, or be able to answer. Instead, I just sighed heavily, took a step into Josh, and rested my head on his chest. I didn't even realize I was cold until Josh's arms wrapped around me, soothing the goose bumps that had just covered my skin.

"It's cold in here," I said into his shirt.

"Why do you have the air up so high?"

"Because it was hot in here when I first got here and I never turned it down. And I sleep hot so I like to have it colder."

"I bet you're hot when you sleep," he said laughing.

I half punched him and tried to pull away but he squeezed me tightly and backed me up against the couch until I fell onto it, him following me.

"Josh. What are you doing?" I exclaimed.

"Nothing," he said nonchalantly. His eyes widened, as did his grin.

He released me from the hug then pinned me down on the couch, and climbed on top of me. His large frame loomed above me. I would have been scared except he was laughing so I laughed too, but it was hard because he was sitting on me. Josh pinned my arms above my head with one hand and his other hand skimmed down the right side of my body sending shivers all over. Then he dug his hand into my side, tickling me. He had me pinned so all I could do was buck my hips wildly.

"Josh," I screamed in laughter.

"Yes?" he replied slyly.

He moved his hand and tickled my other side causing more bucking and laughing. I tried twisting away from him. I hated being tickled. My mom used to do it when I was younger when she was trying to 'bond' with me, but really, it was just another way for her to insult me. She'd say I wasn't fun, or that I was fat, or that I needed to lighten up. Her form of bonding was finding things that she thought were wrong with me and magnified them.

Josh's hand dug into my side again and traveled up to my armpit

"Stop!" I yelled again still laughing but really wanting him to stop. "Let me go."

I bucked and twisted against him, this time I didn't stop. I thrashed my arms and legs wildly until I felt Josh fall off the couch with a loud thud.

"Dang girl. You're tougher than I thought." He huffed and pushed himself to a seated position on the floor.

"I can be when I need to be." I was out of breath so I just stayed sprawled out on the couch mentally slowing down my breath. I heard Josh move beside me, then the couch dipped next to me as he sat up onto the seat. I pulled my knees to my chest and karate chopped my hands in an effort to protect myself from another round of tickling from Josh.

"I'm not going to tickle you again," he said. He was smiling, but his eyes looked sad.

"What's wrong?" I asked.

"You didn't seem to like it." Josh looked down at his hands in his lap.

"The tickling?" I straightened out my legs and pushed myself up to sitting.

"Yeah."

"I don't like it. I hate being tickled." His head snapped up and he squinted his eyes at me.

"I'm sorry." He looked down again.

"Don't be," I said and pushed him lightly.

An awkward silence fell between us. Josh was still and sullen from his failed attempt at whatever the tickling was supposed to be, and I felt bad for making him feel bad.

"Maybe I'll invite Lauren over tonight so I won't be alone," I said breaking the silence. "She did tell me to call her if I ever needed anything."

"You don't want me to stay? And when did you see Lauren?" He genuinely looked upset.

"She dropped me off at your house earlier. She must have been driving to work or something," I said. "I do want you to stay, but your mom didn't seem too keen on that idea."

"I don't care."

"Okay, well I do. I don't want to make her mad. She helped me today and lied to the police for me."

Josh sighed again.

"Stop being moody." I got up off the couch and slipped on one of the two dozen pairs of flip-flops I had lying around the house. I wanted to catch Lauren at the store before her shift was over. I didn't know when it was over, but I wanted to ask her now before it got too late.

I heard Josh chuckle as he stood up from the couch. "Come on, I'll drive you down to the store. Lauren usually works until 2:00."

"Oh, good to know," I said and I opened the front door for him and followed him out.

"We'll figure this out," he said.

"I know."

CHAPTER NINE

It turned out that Lauren had been dying to stay the night at my house. She squealed with excitement, jumped up and down, and hugged Josh and me. There was a strange, wordless exchange that happened between the two of them. She looked at him with wide eyes, and he shook his head as if in a silent no, then she nodded and regained her regular peppiness. The whole thing happened so fast, I would have missed it if I hadn't been looking.

I felt weird having Lauren over because she and I were not close in high school; she was a typical dumb blond, like Karen from *Mean Girls*, but somehow managed to be part of the in-crowd that had tormented me until the day I left. I didn't recall her ever actually saying anything directly to me, but if it was one, it was all. But I had no one else to turn to. Josh needed to be home and at work, Michelle was MIA, so Lauren was the next best thing.

When I answered the door later that evening, Lauren stood there already in her pajamas.

"Hey Lauren," I said.

I was trying really hard to be excited about this. I guess I liked Lauren, but I needed to be careful about what I shared with her. I didn't know if she'd try to get information from me so she could gossip later.

Lauren pushed passed me into the living room. Her arms were full of bags and pillows and a sleeping bag.

"I didn't know what tonight meant," she said and dumped all of her stuff on my couch. "I brought everything."

"What do you mean?"

"Well, is this the part where there's a music montage and you get a makeover and look super-hot and all the boys love you and all the girls are jealous? Or is this when you spill all your deep dark secrets and we cry all night long?" Lauren stared at me expectantly.

Honestly? I didn't even know what to say to her. I just wanted to laugh.

"We can do whatever you want, Lauren. We could do both I guess, although I don't have many deep dark secrets that this whole town doesn't already know about." This was my attempt at humor, but Lauren just laughed uncomfortably.

"I've always wanted to come to your house, but we weren't really friends so it would have been weird, and then there was your mom and my mom didn't want me over here. I bet we could have been friends if everyone wasn't so scared of you." Lauren rambled on as she unpacked her stuff.

"People were afraid of me?" I asked. This surprised me.

"Yeah," she said, setting out some crazy looking curling irons. Who needed five curling irons? "Everyone at school thought you were like drug lord mafia or something."

"Drug lord mafia," I repeated quietly.

"Yeah, but I knew it couldn't be true because you were so nice and just quiet and you did normal things like play softball and you got good grades and you were best friends with Michelle." Lauren stopped short in the middle of her rambling at the mention of Michelle.

She looked up at me from the floor; piles of makeup surrounded her. It looked like she was sorting it all out. I half wondered if she just threw everything she had on her dresser and in the bathroom in a bag and came over.

The awkward silence continued until Lauren shook her head and continued to pull compacts and pencils out of her duffle bag.

"I'm sorry. I know being here must be hard for you. I mean, you left so quickly without being able to say goodbye to anyone, and then people talked about you and your mom for weeks, although I guess you didn't hear any of that which was probably a good thing because the mayor is a huge jerk and probably started all the rumors. Someone even tried to break into your house too, but I don't think they succeeded, the cops like, guarded your house for a while. I don't know why. I know it was searched,"

"Lauren!" I blurted out.

I had just stared at her through her whole rambling rampage, not sure where to interject. She looked at everything but me. She had spit just everything out as if I was holding her at gunpoint.

"Sorry. I ramble when I'm nervous," she smiled guiltily.

"Nervous?"

"Yeah. I mean, I am excited to be here and hang out with you, but all I know about you is what I heard through gossip and it's pretty scary stuff. Like you've killed people, you break bones, you help your mom while she's in jail." Lauren's voice was slowly getting softer and softer as she spoke.

"Okay Lauren. It's secret spilling time," I said

She straightened up and looked directly at me. I had her full attention.

"One: I've never done drugs. Ever. Two: I've never, ever helped my mom with her "business," I air quoted business. "Three: most of the time, I wasn't even at my house. I either went down to the river, to Michelle's house, or just wandered around town. I didn't want any part of what she did." Lauren looked down at her hands in her lap. "Four: the only contact I've had with my mom in the past fifteen months was two weeks ago when my dad told me to go visit her. I will probably never see her again. I am done with that part of my life, she is negative and degrading, and just not a good person."

"I'm sorry," Lauren said.

"Don't be," I countered.

"So why are you here? Why am I here tonight? I know you didn't ask me here because you missed our friendship," she huffed out a small laugh. "And what's up with you and Josh?"

"Those are excellent questions Lauren, but I can't spill everything in the first twenty minutes. Besides, I think I do need a makeover." I smiled at her.

Lauren's eyes lit up. She gathered all her makeup and her five curling irons and asked where the bathroom was.

She and I spent the next three hours in the bathroom, being normal teenagers. Lauren seemed to be in her element. She had surely missed her calling as a beautician. While she worked on me, she talked nonstop and I let her. She recounted everything that happened at school after I left. Every school dance was explained to me in full detail, including what everyone wore and who went home with who at the end of the night.

It sounded exactly like the last few months of my high school experience in Brookhaven. I didn't know anyone, but I got in with a small crowd of friends and I spent most of my time with them.

"So you graduated high school?" Lauren asked. She was putting some finishing touches on my hair.

"Yes. With honors."

"Oh wow." She seemed genuinely impressed by that.

"I didn't sleep with my teachers," I said.

"I figured you didn't. You just didn't seem like that kind of person."

"Like what kind of person."

"Just someone who would do that. Sleep with old people. Trade sex for stuff. I mean, you didn't sleep with any of the boys in our grade, so I couldn't imagine you slept with teachers."

I laughed. Lauren was funny. She didn't seem to have any kind of filter between what she thought and what she said.

"I wasn't. I'm not. I'm not like my mother and never have been."

"I'm sorry," Lauren said again.

"For what?"

"For just now giving you the chance you deserved." She'd stopped fussing with my hair now. "You're a nice girl Jenna, and people are mean."

I just smiled. It was nice to finally have someone to validate you and recognize who you truly are.

"Thanks Lauren." We smiled at each other. "So can I see my hair?"

"Yes! Of course!" she said enthusiastically.

She moved out of the way and handed me a small handheld mirror so I could see the front and back at the same time.

My hair was a mass of curls piled high on top of my head. A few tendrils framed my face. Rhinestone bobby pins crowned the front of the updo like a tiara. She'd done my makeup as well. Light blush covered my cheeks, and purple eye shadow swept over my eyelids that brought out the green in my hazel eyes.

"All dressed up with nowhere to go." I laughed.

"We could go somewhere," she said.

"Like where?"

"The bar in the next town over. They let in eighteen year olds."

I contemplated what she had just told me. I'd been to a few bars in Brookhaven, but it was usually to see a local band play and not to pick up a guy or just be there.

"No, not really," I finally said.

"Okay. It was just an idea. I didn't bring clothes for that anyway."

She fiddled some more with my hair when our conversation died down. We went to the living room again and Lauren started packing up her makeover supplies and I searched for a movie to put in. My phone rang loudly just then making us both jump. I answered it quickly.

"Hello?" I asked. I hadn't looked at the caller ID.

"Jenna!" came Stefanie's voice.

"Stef, hey. What's up?" I walked over to the couch and sank into it.

"Well I haven't heard from you all summer. Is everything okay? How's the town?"

Stefanie knew my whole story and was a big supporter of me finding closure. I was doing well in school, and had healthy friendships with her and Andrew, but she knew something was holding me back.

"Just hanging out with a friend," I said.

"I thought you didn't have any friends back there." She sounded a little jealous.

"I don't. I didn't. Something happened though so I have a friend over."

"A boyfriend?" Now she sounded accusatory.

"No, Stef, not a boy. Her name is Lauren."

Lauren turned to me at the sound of her name and mouthed, 'Who is it'. I shook my head and turned away from her.

"Is there a boy though? What happened?"

"I can't really talk about it right now."

"Okay. I was just wondering what your plans were for the fall. I got a letter about dorm assignments. Are we finding an apartment?"

"Oh, um. All my mail is forwarded to my dad's house. Sorry. I think an apartment is a great idea. More freedom, less communal bathroom."

Stefanie laughed. "Yeah. Okay. Well I'll keep a look out in the newspaper. Andrew said he would too."

"Is he living with us?"

Lauren's head snapped up at the mention of a boy possibly living with me. She scooted closer to try to hear my conversation.

"No, I don't think so. I guess he could." Stefanie replied.

"No, it's okay. I just didn't know if he was thinking about it or something."

"It would save on rent," she pointed out.

"True."

"Well, think about it, and don't forget about me this summer. I'm just wasting away at my parents' while you live it up alone in the middle of nowhere."

"Oh yeah." I rolled my eyes. "Riverview is a hot bed of excitement," I said sarcastically.

"Bye."

"Bye."

I hung up and turned to Lauren. She stared at me like a hungry dog. "What?" I asked.

"Who was that?"

"Stefanie, my roommate at Brookhaven College."

"And you're looking for an apartment together?"

"Yes."

"With a boy?"

"No."

"Who's the boy?" Dang she was nosey.

"It's Andrew." I sighed. I wasn't going to get anything accomplished if I hid that from her. I knew she'd bring it up all night.

"And who is Andrew? Your boyfriend?" She was totally going there.

"Not really."

"Is he hot?"

"Lauren!"

"What? I've seen all the boys here, I need someone new to think about."

We both just laughed. I told her about Andrew and how we met and that we were not dating seriously.

"So what about Josh? What are you two doing?" She was hitting all the hot talking points right now.

"I don't know. I'm not staying here for the long haul. I more than likely won't ever come back here after this summer, and Josh has a good job here so I don't think he'll leave. Ever."

"You're probably right. I'm probably stuck here too. For life." She rolled her eyes.

"Why do you say that?"

"I'm not as smart as you. I didn't graduate with honors or anywhere close to it. I didn't apply to college." She looked down like she was ashamed.

"Lauren, you are smart. Don't say stuff like that. It's never too late to go to college if that's really what you want to do."

"Really?" She looked up at me.

"Yeah. Of course. There are like forty year olds who go to college." Lauren chuckled a little. "Seriously, it's not too late."

"I kind of want to be a hair stylist," she revealed.

"I think that's a great idea. I know of a couple beauty schools in Brookhaven."

"You do?"

"Yes, you get cheap haircuts there from the students so they can practice. I can text Stefanie and get the names if you want"

"Yes, thank you Jenna." She hugged me tightly. "So what are we watching?" she asked.

"I don't know, I hadn't really looked yet."

"Well I brought a scary movie, want to watch it?"

"I love scary movies!"

Lauren popped the DVD into my laptop and we sat back to watch.

It was a scary movie and once it was over, she and I decided to both just sleep in the living room on the couch. She didn't want to sleep alone out here and didn't want to sleep on the floor in my room. I didn't blame her, what if a monster or a killer was under my bed? Irrational thinking was awesome.

We set up pillows and blankets on opposite sides of the couch and switched the DVD's so we were watching *The Little Mermaid*. We needed a happy peaceful movie to watch so we could fall asleep.

***

The next morning my phone beeped at me from under my pillow. It was a text from Josh. Actually, several texts.

How's the night going?
Watching princess movies?
Talking about girly stuff
What are you guys talking about
Call me in the morning.
Let's hang out again soon
I'm coming over tomorrow
I'll be over shortly

The last text was sent less than five minutes ago. I rolled over on the couch onto my back. Lauren was still curled up on her end of the couch, snoring softly. I had to wake her up before Josh got here.

"Lauren," I said softly. Nothing.

"Lauren," I said a little louder. Still nothing.

"Hey," I half yelled. She stirred and opened her eyes. One eyeball twisted to look at me then she sat bolt upright.

"Where am I?" she snuffed.

"You're at my house. It's Jenna. You stayed the night."

"Oh yeah. Sorry. What time is it?" she asked.

"Um." I glanced at my phone. "9:27."

"In the morning?" Lauren said and yawned.

"Yeah."

"Oh okay. Cool. I should probably get going, I have to work at 10:00."

"Oh, wow. Do you want to shower or anything?"

Lauren yawned again. "Yeah that would be great. Thanks."

She rolled off the couch and made her way to the bathroom. I'm not sure she was completely awake yet. I assessed my clothing situation and discovered that I'd slept in my street clothes for the second night in a row. Different clothes, but still not pajamas. I guessed that Josh would be here soon so I went to my room and changed into a pair of jeans and a new t-shirt. I didn't know what was in store for today, but at least I had clothes on.

I walked back out to the living room and caught Josh at the front door before he even knocked. I opened it for him and let him in.

"Is Lauren still here?" he asked without saying hello.

"Hello to you too." I said and folded my arms across my chest.

"Hey, sorry." He leaned down and kissed me softly on the lips.

"She's still here. She's in the shower. She has to work at 10:00."

"Okay."

An awkward silence fell between us. I felt as though he was here waiting for Lauren to leave more than he was to see me. I gathered up all the blankets and pillows and dumped them on the floor in my room.

Lauren was dressed and out of the bathroom before I returned to the living room. She and Josh were speaking to each other in low voices. I crept to the living room slowly so I could maybe hear what they were say.

"Don't worry, I didn't say anything about it," Lauren said. She sounded annoyed though.

"Okay. Good."

"Why is that good? She should know."

"Not yet."

Lauren sighed heavily. What were they talking about? What was it I should know? About my mom? Or Michelle?

"You better get to work anyway. It's almost 10:00."

"It's not like they'd fire me. There's no one else to work there. They'd probably shut the store down if I didn't show up."

"You're being dramatic," Josh laughed.

"Hey guys," I said louder than necessary.

Josh and Lauren took a step back from each other.

"I gotta go." Lauren said quickly. "Thanks for having me over.

Let's do it again soon, okay? I had fun."

"Of course. Text me." I replied. We hugged and she left.

"What was that all about?" I asked Josh.

"What was what?" He asked, feigning innocence.

"Nothing. What are you doing here? Don't you have to work?" I asked.

"Nope. I have the day off."

"I hope not because of me." I'd hate to be the reason he missed out on a paycheck.

"Ah, kind of, but I was already scheduled to have time off soon, so I just took it now."

"I'm not an invalid. I can take care of myself. I don't need a babysitter."

"I know, but aren't you worried about that guy coming back? I know I am."

"No, not really. He didn't find what he was looking for while he was here, so why would he come back?" My logic might be flawed, but he just didn't seem like he'd come back again.

"Well, I also just want to hang out with you. Is that a crime?" He stood in front of me now. His six foot five inch frame towering over my five foot seven.

Not many people tower over me. All of my girlfriends are shorter than I am, and several guys I know are right at eye level or just above me. Not that I really mind a shorter guy, but I liked feeling small in Josh's arms. As if right on cue, he enveloped me in his arms and pulled me tight against his torso. My arms were tucked against my chest so I couldn't hug him back.

I felt safe.

CHAPTER TEN

"So what do you want to do today?" I asked into his chest.

"Hang out here? Or we could go to my place?"

"Your place?" I tried to pull back and look at his face, but I was still pinned to his chest. Not that I was complaining or anything.

We were currently curled up on the couch, my head was on his chest, and my legs were wrapped around his.

"Yeah. My mom is actually gone all day for something. I can't remember now."

"Some random thing?"

"Yeah, like a conference for baking or something."

"They have those?"

"I guess."

"Well, you need to let me go so I can get ready to go."

"You look fine."

"Yeah, well, I need to at least brush my teeth."

"I was wondering what the smell was."

"Shut up," I yelled and wiggled my way away from him. "You're mean." And gave him a playful push.

"Nah, just honest." I gave him a look.

I brushed my teeth and fixed my hair so I didn't look like I'd slept on half a couch all night long, even though I had. Never doing that again. I secretly snagged my favorite movie from the DVD pile, there was no way I could sit through another action/car/robot movie. He'd just have to deal with my choice.

I locked the house up behind me and we made the short drive to his house in his truck with the windows rolled down. His house was quiet and empty when we walked in. No lights were on, but all the curtains were open so the mid-morning sun streamed in through the windows.

"Follow me," Josh said.

I followed him through the living room and down a steep flight of stairs where we both had to duck to avoid a low ceiling at the bottom. We were in Josh's room. The actual ceiling was only a few inches above his head, and if he wasn't careful, he'd knock his head against the light fixture.

Josh flopped down on his belly onto his bed and looked at me like I should follow. The scenarios I'd thought up in my head of what Josh and I would do in his or my bed did not include movie watching or talking. I was suddenly nervous.

Josh and I dated when we were sixteen and while he wasn't the only boy I dated, I didn't date much after him. In fact, I didn't have another boyfriend while I lived in Riverview. Most of the boys in school thought I was like my mom and wanted in my pants, so I avoided them like the plague.

When I moved to Brookhaven with my dad, no one knew me. I was the new girl and I'd come for the last half of my senior year. It wasn't really enough time to form relationships with anyone. I did fall into a small group of friends. They took me in my first day when they saw me looking lost in the cafeteria. I was soon introduced to Bryan. He was tall and quiet. We went on a few dates, we kissed, and we made out in movie theaters. We went to Prom together and at an after party we had bad sex. I never talked to him again after that. There were only a few weeks left in school and so I'd thrown myself into studying and finals and that was it for Bryan.

When I started in college, Andrew was the first and only boy I talked to. He and Stefanie were the only two people I really ever hung out with last year. Andrew and I stayed platonic for a while until Stef found a boyfriend and begged us to double date with her. Sex just hadn't happened between us yet.

I followed Josh's lead and sat on the edge of the bed and crossed my legs. My heart skipped a beat and butterflies tried to escape my mid-section when the side of his body touched my back. It wasn't even in a sexual way, but just the close proximity of our bodies was making my heart race, and my skin prickle with delicious goosebumps.

"So what are we watching tonight?" he asked and ran his finger up and down my bare arm. I involuntarily shivered at his touch.

"You okay?" he asked. It was a whisper in my ear.

"Yeah," I barely whispered. I cleared my throat and said, "just cold." Which was a total lie.

Josh sat up and joined me on the edge of the bed.

"We don't have to do anything," he said.

I was glad he'd said that. I knew I wanted to be with him, I just wasn't sure I was ready to be with him in that capacity. My conversation with Lauren last night, and Stefani calling and bringing up Andrew had my mind racing.

"So what are we going to watch?" he asked, changing the subject.

I seriously contemplated forgoing the romantic comedy I had stashed in my purse and watching an action movie, but I hadn't watched *Notting Hill* since I'd been back in Riverview and I usually watched it weekly. Okay, daily. I reached into my purse and pulled out the movie and handed it to him.

"*Notting Hill*," he read slowly. "What is that about?"

"It's about a bookstore owner and a movie star who fall in love."

"Really?" he didn't sound too enthusiastic about it.

"Yeah." I looked at him.

"Really?" he said again but smiling this time.

"It's my favorite movie. We had to watch *XXX* last time and it was awful."

"What? That movie was awesome."

"Well this one is too." Josh sighed, but got up anyway and loaded the disc into his DVD player and switched on the TV.

"Want some popcorn?" he asked. He was already at the stairs so I just nodded my head.

Josh's bed stuck out diagonally from the TV so the end of the bed was closest to it. I repositioned myself so that I was leaning against the head of the bed with his pillows behind my back. His pillows had the same woody, pine scent I always smelled on him. I wanted to roll over and bury my face in the bed and wrap myself up in the comforter. I didn't though. He'd be back down with the popcorn soon and it would be awkward to explain why I'd crawled underneath his covers.

When he returned, he smiled at me when he saw me and joined me on his bed. We snuggled close to each other, eventually he had his arm around me, and my head was on his chest. It was kind of awkward and uncomfortable with his arm snaked around my back but I didn't want to move and make him think I didn't want to be near him. I know it sounded stupid.

The entire movie, I kept thinking about how easy it would be to just straddle him right now and kiss him passionately to get something started, but my body just didn't move when I told it to. Before I knew it, the movie was over, Hugh and Julia were together, and I was still sitting uncomfortably next to Josh.

"So did you like it?" I asked when I flipped the TV to MTV after movie ended.

"I liked the weird Welsh guy. His shirts were funny."

I just laughed. I was a little disappointed that he hated my favorite movie, but he tried to like it for me and that made me happy.

"Well at least you've watched it now and you don't have to ever see it again."

"I'd watch it again if it meant I got to be with you." His face was dead serious. I almost laughed because it's not like his statement was some life changing, sentimental statement. I just stared back at him, waiting for him to make a move.

"Jenna, I want to kiss you again." This guy knew how to be serious. He could get me all worked up with just one sentence.

"I want you to kiss me again." I breathed, because that's all I could do. The anticipation was killing me.

He leaned over me, positioning one knee between my legs and the other leg was braced on the headboard. He loomed over me. I lifted my hands and placed them around his back and pulled him down to me. His mouth crashed down onto mine, leaving me breathless immediately. I slipped my hands down his back and under his shirt, pushing it up over his shoulders. He tugged it over his head, tossed it on the floor, and smiled at me. His hands were on my waist pulling my shirt up too. I leaned forward and allowed him to pull it off. I usually wore two layers, a cami and a shirt, but today I just had a t-shirt on so, now I was lying beneath him in just my bra and shorts.

Josh smiled at me again before he leaned down and kissed me softly on the cheek, then across my jawline and down my neck. I wrapped my arms around him again and let my fingers graze the smooth skin of his back. He moaned quietly and arched his back in response to my touch. I didn't know if he wanted to touch me in the same way, but he slid his hand under my back and lifted me to him. I clung to him as he pulled me on to his lap so I was straddling him. He proceeded to lightly brush his fingers up and down my spine that sent tingles and sparks of desire to my core.

I cupped his face in my hands and straightened his face so he had to look at me, fully aware that while my back was arched, my chest was pressing into his. He glanced down a few times at my breasts and it made me giggle. I leaned in to kiss him and when our lips met, he closed his eyes.

"Keep your eyes open," I whispered. His eyes flew open again and stayed on mine. "Don't close them, I want you to watch me."

I kissed him softly again on his lips and watched his piercing blue eyes darken with each pass my lips made against his. His breath quickened, as did mine until he slipped his tongue between my lips, meeting mine. I closed my eyes at this point and combed my fingers through his shaggy blond hair. I pressed his face closer to mine as he pressed my hips into his. I gasped at this motion and it spurred him on. He grabbed me behind my knees and pulled me closer to him. My foot brushed something hard at the foot of the bed, but I ignored it. All I could think about was being closer to Josh. His mouth left mine and trailed kisses down my neck and across my chest then down between my breasts. I threw my head back and let him hold me in place at my waist as I held onto the back of his neck. I readjusted myself when Josh's hands found their way up to my bra. He fiddled with the hooks and I moved my feet under his thighs. My foot brushed the hard thing on the bed again and all too suddenly I realized what it was.

The volume on the TV cranked up to the max startling us both. My foot must have been pressing the volume button on the remote. I jumped up off Josh and the bed and pushed the power button on the television. I stood across the room from Josh, staring at him while I attempted to catch my breath. Not just from the volume of the TV, but from our steamy make out session. I was about to let him take off my bra and show him my boobs.

"You okay?" he asked.

"Yeah. Are you?" I asked back.

"Yeah." He got up from the couch and met me by the TV.

He took my hand, pulling me to him and wrapping his arms around me. His skin burned hot against mine causing me relive the last five minutes in my head. He must be thinking about it too because he leaned in and kissed me once on the lips before retrieving his discarded shirt and pulling it on over his head. I looked around for mine too. He found it first and tossed it to me.

I can't say I wasn't a little disappointed to see his shirt slip back on. Stupid television.

"What now?" I asked.

"Another movie?"

"Sure. I guess. We can watch something about cars or robots," I said playfully.

"I have robot cars,"

"Even better."

We spent the rest of the day watching movies. He fixed ham and cheese sandwiches for lunch, and we snacked on chips and popcorn during the movies.

"Hey, remember when I said I wanted to take you out again?" he asked after the fourth car movie of the day. He did not have any romantic comedies, so I was stuck with his boy movies.

"Yeah," I replied.

"Well, I want to take you somewhere."

"Where?" I asked.

"It's a surprise."

"I hate surprises." I shook my head and looked down. I really did hate surprises. When I was eight, my mom decided she wanted to throw me a surprise birthday party. It backfired epically-no one came. I half believed that it was because it was my mom and no one wanted their kids at our house, but in the back of my mind I wondered if it was really because no one liked me.

"Just let me take you out."

"Okay, when?" I laughed.

"How about tomorrow? It's Friday."

"It is Friday."

"I want to show you something," he smiled playfully.

"And what you want to show me happens on Fridays?"

"No, it can happen any night. I was just stating that it was Friday."

I laughed again. "Okay. Well sure. It's not like I have something else planned."

"Great. I'll pick you up around 8:00."

"What should I wear?" I asked

"Whatever you want."

"Well you're no help."

"Jeans and a t-shirt. You look sexy like that."

He gripped the back of my neck with one hand and twisted his fingers into my hair.

"Is that right?" I asked.

I kissed his forehead. When I pulled away, he pushed me back to him and captured my mouth in his. I guess he couldn't wait any longer. I let out a groan. He smiled into the kiss and flicked his tongue over mine then kissed me again.

"You should take me home," I said ending our kiss.

"Why?" He kissed me again.

"I just want to be home. I need to shower." I kissed him again. I couldn't seem to get enough of his lips.

"You can shower here. Better yet, I need to shower too. We could save water."

As enticing as that sounded, I didn't know when Mrs. Riley would be home, and having her find me naked with her son in the shower was not something I'd like to live through. I still remembered what she did for me a few days ago and I didn't want to lose her trust and respect. Sleeping with Josh in my house was one thing, but doing it under her roof was unacceptable to me.

"I can't, your mom."

"What about my mom?"

"I like her, and I respect that this is her house, and I don't want to lose her trust." I said making my thoughts known to him.

"I see that," he said. "Is Lauren staying the night again?"

"No, I don't think so."

He frowned. I didn't know why he was so unhappy about this. I really could defend myself. I had tossed the sweaty guy off. No one had actually broken into my house. He'd knocked and I had stupidly let him in. It wouldn't happen again.

"I don't like you being alone," Josh said. Concern played on his face.

"I'll be fine," I replied.

"Even with a crazy person out there?"

"Well he hasn't been back so…" I didn't know what else to say. I couldn't stay at the Riley's forever.

"I know."

"Just take me home, okay?"

He kissed me again then grabbed my hand and led me back up the stairs.

It was amazing to me how quickly our relationship had progressed. I missed him when he wasn't around. I craved his touch and kiss. I thought about him all the time. I thought about what we would do together and where we would do things. Sometimes it was sex, but I really just liked being with him and I wanted to spend more time with him.

CHAPTER ELEVEN

Josh picked me up promptly at eight. I had chosen to wear my dark blue jeans and a grey distressed t-shirt with rhinestones on the shoulders. It was a random impulse buy at the mall with Stefanie last fall. It wasn't really my style, but it was cute. I wore my favorite, almost worn out turquoise suede flats. Josh was in jeans and a baby blue polo that accentuated his tanned skin and piercing blue eyes. His blond hair was mussed up just the way I liked it. I resisted the urge to run my fingers through it. He wouldn't mind if I did though. The cab of his truck was filled with the scent of his cologne. It was sweet, warm, and clean and set off every sex trigger in my body. I wasn't sure I would make it through this night.

"Hey there," he said. He had helped me into his truck, raced around the front of it, and hopped in his side.

"Hey," I said when he shut his door. "Where are we going?"

"Sonic, then it's a surprise."

"Sonic? The drive in? Really?"

"Hell yeah babe. Half priced shakes after 8 pm."

"Babe? We have nicknames now?" I wasn't so sure I liked it.

"I guess. I just kind of made it up."

"I see. Well do I have to think of one for you?"

"Stud." he said slowly like he was contemplating whether or not to even say it.

"Oh geez."

We drove on down the highway listening to the radio loudly and singing along. Living in a small town surrounded by farmland and other small towns severely limited our selection of restaurants to go to. Sonic, Pizza Hut, a Chinese place, and a few mom and pop places were about it.

It was a busy night at Sonic. We ate at one of the tables and watched minivans full of yelling kids pull in and out of the stalls. Josh had ordered us both hamburgers with French fries, chocolate shakes and two sodas. I didn't have the heart to tell him I didn't like chocolate, so I drank half of it and pretended I was too full to finish. I don't think he was too upset because he happily slurped down the rest.

The night air cooled as the sun dipped below the horizon, which really meant it was now eighty degrees instead of one hundred. We got back in the truck and I waited expectantly as Josh started the engine and turned on the A/C.

"Now what?"

"Now, you have to wear a blindfold."

"What? Why?" Blindfolding was not part of the deal here.

"Yeah. I told you it was surprise. I don't want you to see where we're going. It might ruin it."

"It's getting dark out; I can barely see anything anyway."

"Humor me, please."

"There aren't many places I don't know about here."

"Please?"

"Okay fine."

I let him tie the blindfold on then I sat back against the back of the seat and waited for him to pull out of the parking lot. We pulled out of the parking lot and rumbled down the old highway. At least I think we did. Frigid air blasted from the vents. I desperately wanted to open my window and feel the blazing hot wind against my skin, but Josh had blindfolded me and I wasn't sure where the window roller downer thing was. I wasn't even sure if there was a window roller downer thing or if I had to push a button. I'd just be flailing my hand around until it landed on something familiar. That would be stupid. Moreover, I didn't want to look stupid in front of Josh. Even though we had known each other for years, and we've had a few steamy make out sessions, it was different now. We had been spending more time together, more intentional time, he's at my house all the time, he worried and cared about me and I, him. I had found myself thinking about him all the time, and daydreaming about a future together even though I didn't plan on staying in Riverview.

I sighed to myself. He was within arm's reach, but he felt like a million miles away because I had this stupid blindfold. I wanted to touch him or hold his hand, but finding his hand would be impossible so I just resigned to sitting quietly in my own little corner of the truck.

"I need a drink." I said after a time. "Can I have some of yours?" I asked. I was suddenly thirsty

"Sure, just grab it." Ugh, really? That would mean more flailing of hands. I had no idea where the cup holders were.

"Can you hand it to me?"

"Nope."

"Jerk." He chuckled. "Can I take off the blindfold?"

He chuckled again. "Nope."

"Jerk."

I leaned forward in the passenger's seat and felt around to my left for cup holders. Nothing. I felt lower between the seats.

"Dang it! Where is it?" I let the annoyance show in my voice.

Josh was laughing at me again. I should have just kept my drink. Instead, I had tossed it after we'd finished eating. He said he was taking me somewhere after dinner, a surprise, and I didn't want to have to pee every five minutes. Now I was dying of thirst and I really needed a drink.

"It's between your legs, isn't it?" I knew the answer before he said anything.

"Maybe," he still had a laugh in him.

"That's okay; I don't want your penis soda."

"What?" He burst out with a laugh.

"I don't want to reach over there."

"My penis is in my pants and nowhere near the soda."

I really needed a drink.

I unbuckled my seatbelt, scooted into the middle seat, and buckled the lap belt. Josh breathed in deeply and coughed as he let it out. He shifted in his seat, shaking the ice in the cup. Damn it. I was going to have to reach blindly between his legs. Fine, I could play games too.

I placed my hand on his upper thigh. This caused him to tense immediately. Good. I slid it down to his knee and back up, then squeezed it down to his inner thigh. I felt the cup against the back of my hand, so I swiped it.

"You are bad," he said.

"You have no idea."

I heard him suck in a breath and gun the engine. I was thrown back against my seat at the acceleration.

We rode in silence after that, so I left my hand resting on his leg while I sipped on his soda. The radio fuzzed randomly here and there. I could tell it was getting darker; the sun wasn't blazing through the window anymore. Josh had finally turned down the air conditioning. The road had gotten bumpier too. Maybe a dirt road or an old pot holed one?

The radio fuzzed in clear on a song we both recognized. I would turn it up, but again, flailing hands.

"I love this song!" Josh said and turned up the volume.

"Really? Why?" I liked it too.

"It's a love song. They are talking about being in love."

"Actually, they aren't."

"Yes they are. He's saying he misses it when she was his," he sang along to the words to reiterate his point. "See, you are mine again. It is a love song. This should be our song."

"No. They're talking about a lost love and remembering a time when they were together."

"Well I never want to forget us together."

I had to admit, even though he was wrong about the song, his sentiment was sweet.

We bumped along the road for a little while longer, turning here and there. I wondered if he was trying to throw me off somehow by making random turns. It worked if he was; I had no idea where we could be.

"Where are we?" I asked when we finally stopped.

"We're here," he teased.

"I gathered that. Can I take the blindfold off?"

"Not yet."

Without another word, he exited the truck, leaving me alone in the dark. He must have been getting stuff from the back because the tailgate slammed open then closed, rattling the whole vehicle. The passenger's side door popped open. Josh grabbed my arm, pulled me gently across the seat, and lifted me out of the truck.

"Now?"

"Almost," his whisper sent shivers through my mind and body. I wanted him. There was no denying it anymore.

His hands fell from my back to my hand as he pulled me along beside him. It smelled sweet and green, like honeysuckles, and a little of damp earth. The familiar trickling of water told me instantly where we were. The cool night breeze whipped around me and I sighed. The heavy stalks of corn shivered and the leaves shook in the wind. Josh had brought me to my favorite place. The river.

"Are we at the river?"

"Yes. How'd you guess?" He sounded a little sad.

"I can hear and smell it. I can smell the cornfield. Are you going my way to get there?

"Yes." He was leading through the maze of corn, our own secret mission.

"I used to come out here after school to get away sometimes," I blurted out. I'm not sure why I decided to share that bit of history.

"Away from me?" He stopped. He moved in front of me and lifted the blindfold. He was face to face with me. His blue eyes stared into my hazel, not that I could make out the color of his eyes in the pitch-blackness around us.

"Sometimes. When we broke up it was hard on me."

"I'm sorry."

"For what?"

"For what happened while you were here. I liked you Jenna, but it was just an awkward situation. I was an idiot. That was not how you deserved to be treated."

"It's okay." I looked down at what I thought might be my feet. It was hard to tell in the dark.

"It's not okay." He lifted my chin with his fingers until I was looking into his eyes again. There wasn't even a moon. There was no light.

"Okay." It was all I could think to say.

"Come on."

He grabbed my hand, turned on a flashlight and continued to lead me through the cornrows. The light of the flashlight bounced along the path ahead of us. The rushing of the river was getting louder and the cornstalks were thinning out until they disappeared completely.

"We're here," I said.

He let go of my hand so he could spread the blanket out and I noticed he had two. He set the cooler down in one corner and the flashlight on top of it. I looked around and we were on the bank of the river, just off to the side of the muddy area. Grass grew thick and wild here.

"I come here too but at night." He pulled me down onto the first blanket, then threw the second one around his shoulders and pulled me to him so I was leaning against his chest, his mouth close to my ear so his breath tickled.

"I'm afraid of the dark," I admitted.

"What? No you're not." Josh was actually laughing at me.

"I am, actually," I said dead serious and turned to look in his eyes. Well, look the best I could because it was so dark and I could not see an inch in front of my face.

"You don't have to be scared with me, Jenna." I thought again that he might kiss me but he didn't. He just pulled me back against him and wrapped his arms and the blanket around me. I settled in and let him hold me. I did feel safe with him.

"Watch," he whispered.

I looked up into the night sky to see the billions of stars that dotted the sky. I was not good with astronomy, but I was able to find Orion, one of the dippers, and I could see the Milky Way. As I was star gazing something streaked across the sky in my peripheral vision.

"Did you see that?" Josh squeezed me with excitement.

"I think so." I wasn't exactly sure what I was looking for to be honest. I knew geese migrated through this area, but I couldn't imagine Josh would bring me out here at night to see them. Especially since I had an unnatural fear of birds flying over my head.

It happened again, but this time I saw it. A shooting star.

"Wow," I said in wonderment.

"There's a meteor shower tonight and there is no moon so

we'll be able to see all of them."

"That's amazing. How did you know about this? It's so beautiful."

"My mom told me."

"Ah. You're mom planned the date," I teased.

He rocked me in his arms a little and laughed.

I settled back into Josh's chest and rested my head against one of his shoulders. The longer we sat amongst the sweet corn, the more meteors started to fall. They shot across the sky in all directions, some with long tails, and some with shorter tails, all leaving glittering trails behind them.

We sat wrapped up in each other for over an hour watching the stars fall, but it felt like no time at all. The air was warm but the breeze was cool, betraying the fact that it would probably be a scorcher tomorrow. I leaned back further into Josh's broad chest and rested my head against his shoulder. Josh shifted behind me and lowered his head so we were touching cheeks. His warm breath fluttered against my neck. White-hot liquid desire seeped into my veins and traveled throughout my body. I shifted against him this time and he tightened his arms even more around me, then brushed his hands up and down my arms. I wanted him to kiss me.

God must have been listening because Josh's soft lips pressed gently against my exposed neck. He kissed me repeatedly, following the curve of my neck down to my collarbone. I unfolded my hands from the blanket and caressed his rough, lightly stubbled face. He pressed harder against my neck causing me to gasp with desire. I turned toward him and guided his face to mine. He hesitated, hovering centimeters in front of me. I moved in closer, brushing my lips against his. Still he paused. Was he teasing me?

If he was, it was driving me crazy. I sat on my knees, leaned forward, and placed both hands on either side of his face, watching him watch me the whole time. I know he had to know what I was doing.

"Kiss me," I whispered, giving him one last chance. He breathed heavily and smiled but still did not move. He was teasing me.

I leaned in, kissed him once on his full lips, and pulled away. I moved in again and captured his lips in mine, sucking his bottom lip gently when I pulled away. Again, I pressed my lips to his, this time he responded. He pushed his tongue against my lips and I let him in. My tongue met his and it was heaven. Shots of want and desire coursed through me. I rose up and pulled Josh closer to me, sliding my hands down his neck and over his shoulders. His arms wrapped around my waist and he held me to him, kissing me hard, and his tongue passing over mine.

"Jenna," Josh breathed. His body was tense and I could tell he wanted me as much as I wanted him. The way he said my name, as if it was the last name he would ever say, sent me over the edge. I leaned into him further, my hands in his hair, his hands in mine. He pushed me to the ground and climbed on top of me. He straddled me and I could feel what I was doing to him.

"I want you Jenna."

"I was--" was all I managed before his mouth claimed mine again.

I wrapped my arms and legs around him and pressed my hips to his. I wanted him to keep kissing me as he did last night. I wanted his body close to mine. I doubted we would go any further than this out here, but we both wanted more, I felt it in the way he touched me.

"Jenna, stop." Josh breathed into my mouth, mirroring my thoughts.

"Why?" I asked and continued to kiss him. Just because I was thinking about stopping didn't mean I wanted to. And we were so close, I just didn't want to lose it.

"We shouldn't."

"Why?" I asked again. Still kissing him. I wanted him to say it.

"I don't know. Not here. Not now. Not yet." He breathed again

"Okay," I said against my better judgment. "Eventually we're going to have to do it you know?" I wanted to keep going. I wanted Josh. Who cared if we were outside in the dirt in a cornfield? It was a warm night, the stars were gorgeous, and they were falling--like I was falling for him.

Josh lifted himself off me and extended his hand to me. He pulled me up to standing then turned around quickly and opened the cooler.

"What's in the cooler?" I asked.

"I actually brought cake," he said.

"Cake?"

"Yeah. I know it was your birthday earlier this month before you came here."

"You remembered my birthday?"

"Yeah. I'll always remember your birthday."

Josh leaned over and kissed me softly at the corner of my eye. I shivered at his touch.

"You cold?" he asked

"No. I just do that when you touch me."

After our cake, we sat for a while longer, just gazing up at the stars. Every so often Josh would kiss the side of my face, or the top of my head. I felt like I could stay this way forever. Eventually though, he said it was time to go so we packed up and climbed back into the truck. I checked my phone and it was almost three in the morning.

"Do I have to be blindfolded on the way home?" I teased.

"Not unless you want to be." The way he said that made me want him to blindfold me just to see what he would do to me. Instead, I sat in the center seat so I could be touching him the whole ride home.

Josh drove me back to my house in silence. We didn't take near as many turns on the way back as we did on the way there. He parked the truck in front of my house and turned off the engine.

"Do you want to come inside?" I asked, not looking at him.

"No, Jenna. I have to work all day tomorrow."

"If you didn't have to work, would you come in?"

"Yes," he said quickly.

"Okay." I opened the door and the dome light illuminated his face. He looked sad. "Are you okay?"

"Yeah." He laughed and ran his fingers through his hair. "I'm good. I'll see you later Jen."

"Bye."

Josh slid his hand behind my neck and pulled me into a deep kiss. His tongue wrapped around mine then slid back, leaving me wanting more. But he released his grip on me and I hopped out of the cab of the truck.

The house was quiet and empty. I stripped my clothes on my way back to my room. I curled up under the patchwork quilt I had dug out of the hallway linen closet and replayed the night. I was falling for Josh, that was a no brainer, and I felt like he was into me too. Why was my summer becoming so complicated? I slammed my hands down into the bed in mock frustration.

CHAPTER TWELVE

I was going to disconnect my phone. Andrew had called twice, Stefanie as well. It wasn't even eight in the morning. It was the Tuesday after my starry night date with Josh. He had had to work all weekend from sun up to sun down. Farmers were not kidding when they said they worked long hours. He'd texted me all weekend though, to remind me about our kisses and to tell me I was beautiful. But I guess there were some water lines that needed fixed so he had to work extra to get it done quickly. It hadn't rained in weeks so I knew the farmers were hurting for water.

The phone rang again and I ignored it. It immediately rang again so I picked up and answered exasperatedly. Not that I was busy doing anything, but I just was not in the mood to talk.

"Hello?" I huffed.

"Jenna."

Oh God. It was my mom. What the heck did she want?

"Hi Mom," I said cautiously.

"How's everything going?" She sounded too cheery and not like my mom.

"Fine, Mom."

"Good. I just wanted to check on you. See what you've been doing. Have you had any visitors?"

I knew then that she wanted to see if her buddy had stopped by for the drugs. "Why do you care, Mom?" Two could play at this game.

"I'm just wondering Sweetie. Just wondering who's traipsing through my house." She gave a laugh like she didn't care, but I knew her too well.

"I'm pretty sure this is Dad's house."

"Whatever," her voice was clipped and the concern had changed to truth. "Well, has anyone stopped by?"

"Josh Riley comes by every day."

"Anyone else?"

She was obviously not concerned about me having boys over.

"Mom. Get to the point," I was way past annoyed with this conversation.

"I sent a friend. It wasn't obvious when he came over?" She sounded genuinely confused.

"Some random guy in a business suit shows up on my doorstep sweaty and trying to sell me vacuums! He forced his way in and attacked me Mom! That's who you sent to the house."

"Oh." She didn't seem surprised, just a little confused.

I waited a beat before realizing that she wasn't going to say anything more.

"Really? All you have to say is 'oh'? You are unbelievable. You sent some random guy to the house where I am staying alone to get drugs you left behind and you don't even care that your daughter could have died?"

"I didn't send a random person over there. I sent a very specific person over, but he sent someone else. And you're not dead, so I don't have to worry."

I hung up the phone. She couldn't care less if I died. I didn't want to hear anything else she had to say. She deliberately called someone to come over to this house and collect her drugs. She knew I was here alone. Who the hell did she call? It wasn't the sweaty vacuum man. I slid the screen over on my phone, unlocked it, and sent a text to Josh.

Hey, you busy

Nope. Just waiting for cows to move. What's up

My mom called

Oh yeah

She called someone about the drugs, but it wasn't the man who came to my door

What do you mean, he responded.

I mean she just asked me if I'd had any visitors at the house and when I mentioned the sweaty vacuum guy she said she didn't send him

Then who

She said she sent a specific person over but that he sent someone else

There was a short pause before he responded. I racked my

brain for possibilities, but I just could not think straight. I was so mad at my mom.

The mayor? He finally pinged back to me.

Of course! She had called Mayor Banks and he had sent the poor guy to do his dirty work. Knowing my mother though, she was probably supplying him too. This sucked so badly!

Yes, it was him. I know it

How do you know

Because he doesn't want to be involved in this stuff again, but he wants his drugs

You want to tell the police?

Tell them what? We have no proof that he has any hand in this

I don't know Jen. I gotta go, the cows are moving

I sat angry on the couch for over an hour and tried to think of a ways to get the mayor in trouble. Nothing. I'd come up with nothing. Other than the evidence from fifteen months ago, there was nothing to connect him to the drugs my mom still had at the house. And there was zero evidence connecting him to the man who showed up at my door and attacked me.

I could not be in the house anymore. Just thinking about the sweaty man made me paranoid. I kept looking over at the door expecting him to be there. I didn't even know what to do though. I thought about going to the river, but I wasn't sure I wanted to be by myself right now. I would just dwell on the whole situation and make myself feel worse. I looked at my phone as if it was going to tell me what to do. It told me everything else in the world. I slid the screen across to open it and noticed I had a text message. It was from Andrew.

call me

I really did not want to talk to Andrew. I was so confused about everything right now. Michelle was MIA and didn't seem to even want to see me. She was half the reason I'd come back. Josh and I were doing well, but I was leaving at the end of August. I needed direction. I needed someone to tell me what to do next. The only thing I was sure of was that I was done with my mother. She was erased from my memories starting now. She'd been nothing but trouble my whole life. I wasn't like her and I didn't want to be.

The phone chimed at me to notify me of a new text. It wasn't Andrew this time though. It was Josh.

I'm going to be late. Meet me at my house

Well there you go. My phone had just told me what to do next.

I drove down to the Riley's house instead of walk. My rationale behind that was I'd stay cool in my car and not be in the heat for long. Good thoughts, except my car was boiling hot and didn't cool off before I got to their house despite having the air conditioning on full blast. I was sweating buckets before I reached their door. We needed some rain to get rid of this humidity.

Mrs. Riley answered the door with a smile.

"Jenna, what are you doing here?"

"I don't want to be at my house right now."

"Is everything okay?"

"I'm not sure."

"Come in," she said.

She moved aside so I could enter. Her house smelled amazing. Either she was burning a very convincing candle or she was baking. I guessed the latter when she walked past me into the kitchen.

"What are you making?" I asked. I followed her into the kitchen and took a seat at the table facing her while she moved around the kitchen.

"Apple pie," she responded.

"Smells good, Mrs. Riley"

"It's Josh's favorite."

"I remember."

"Do you?"

"Yeah. You used to make apple pie every Sunday. He'd always invite me over for dinner because he said you made the best apple pie in the state, possibly the country."

"He said that?"

"Yeah."

She gathered more apples and brought them to the table. She handed me a knife and a few apples as she sat down and we sliced them together.

"Why didn't you ever come for dinner?" she asked.

"Um." I wasn't sure how to answer this. I knew my mother had slept with her husband and I knew that she knew it too. "I don't know. I just never got around to it."

"You and Josh have been friends for a long time."

"Yes. Since like second grade, I think."

"I'm sorry I wasn't more welcoming to you." Her face was set in a slight frown. Not a mad frown, a sad one.

"It's okay. I knew why."

"Did you?"

Mrs. Riley had stopped slicing apples and was staring intently at me, the knife still in her hand. I stared back at her until her face softened. She wasn't angry, just hurt, but not by me.

"I'm sorry," I said finally.

"Oh honey. Don't say that. I should be the one who is sorry." She stood up and walked around the table to me. I stood up too.

"Why?"

"Jenna," she started and put her hands on my shoulders. "I let what happened between my husband and your mother determine how I felt about you. I didn't want Josh around you because he was all I had left after his father left."

I had no idea how to take this. Mrs. Riley was never directly rude to me, but I always got the feeling that she didn't want me around. Now I knew why Josh had broken up with me. I always kind of assumed that was the reason, just another way my mom ruined my life here.

"It's okay."

"No honey, it's not okay. The way I treated you is something that I have regretted for a long time. I knew Josh had strong feelings for you, but like I just said, I was afraid he'd leave me after he graduated from high school and I was jealous of what you two had. And to be honest, I was afraid you'd end up like your mom. I didn't want that for Josh."

Tears brimmed in her eyes. Her candid admission made me feel closer to her now for some reason.

"Mrs. Riley, I know what this town thought of me and my mother, I'm not like her in any capacity."

"I know, but you didn't deserve that life and you didn't deserve the way I treated you." Her tears had fallen now and she wiped them away with the heel of her hand.

She pulled me into a hug. I was ready for it but it still felt strange. My mom never hugged me affectionately; the only people who had were Michelle, Andrew, and Josh and none of them were parental figures. I hugged her back.

"What's going on?"

Mrs. Riley and I ended our hug and looked over to Josh. He had walked in without us knowing and caught us in our strange embrace.

"Jenna and I were just having a heart to heart, that's all," Mrs. Riley said wiping away the rest of her tears.

"About what we talked about earlier?" Josh asked and looked at me.

"No. I haven't said anything about that."

"About what?" Mrs. Riley asked.

"Jenna thinks the man who attacked her was sent by her mother."

"I know he was sent by her. But I think she's working through Mayor Banks," I said completing Josh's statement.

"Mayor Banks? Why do you think that?" she asked

"Because the mayor is a jackass."

Josh snorted out a laugh at that.

"I don't think that will convince the police," Mrs. Riley said.

"It won't. I sat for an hour on the couch trying to figure something out, but I haven't thought of anything. Did I tell you I ran into him on the second day I was here? He was at Miller's Market. He cornered me in the soap aisle and ranted about how awful of a person I was and how I ruined his family and that he hopes I leave soon. Oh, and to never try to contact his family. I hadn't even said anything to him at all. He just went off on me."

Josh and his mom exchanged knowing glances.

"Is there something going on that I should know about?" These glances that Josh keeps exchanging with people, namely Lauren and his mom, were annoying me. What was he keeping from me? Was it about Mayor Banks and his family? Did it involve my mom, because if it did, I should know.

They looked at each other again.

"No honey. Nothing you need to concern yourself with right now."

I wasn't satisfied with her answer, but I had more pressing matters to attend to than potential secrets. I'd grill Josh later when we were alone.

"We'll figure this out," Josh said.

Just then the oven timer went off. Josh looked at me and smiled.

"Mom, I don't want Jenna to go home tonight. Especially after the phone call with her mom. What if she's called the mayor again?"

Mrs. Riley removed the pie from the oven and set it on a cooling rack. She pressed a knife to the top and steam billowed out.

"I think Jenna could stay here for a night," she said then sprinkled sugar on top of the pie.

"Really?" Josh and I said in unison.

"Yes. I'm worried about her too. I want you to be safe. And now that we know your mother is still able to contact the people she's done business with, who knows who else could show up."

I knew Mrs. Riley was feeling guilty about how she'd treated me in the past. I wondered if I could sneak downstairs to be with Josh. I quickly dismissed that thought. How disrespectful would that be? She was opening her house to me a second time. She felt bad for me and my situation and she just wanted me to be safe. Now that we knew who was behind the attack and that he would doing anything he could to cover it up, my safety really could be at risk. Who knew what the mayor would do to me and even worse, what he'd do to cover it up.

"Don't get all gooey eyed over there. Jenna sleeps on the pull out bed in the living room. Upstairs. You," she pointed at Josh with the knife she was holding, "stay in the basement." She was smiling as she said this, but I knew she was serious. Josh was just flat out laughing.

"Okay mom," he said and rolled his eyes. He then turned to

me and said, "Let's go get your things."

"I'll have dinner ready when you get back."

With that, Josh and I left. I wasn't sure how to feel about this whole situation. I was scared again obviously. I was scared before too, but now that it was not some arbitrary person who attacked me, but the mayor sending out people for my mom, I felt like it had just gotten way more complicated. Then there was the fact that we had no proof about any of it. I knew in my heart that the mayor was working with my mom and was behind all of this, but I had nothing to go on but a gut feeling.

We took his truck up to my house. I packed quickly while Josh waited on the couch. I packed an old duffle bag with a couple pairs of shorts, a few tops and underwear and flip-flops. I also grabbed a black bra and matching boy short-style panties. If tonight was going to be like last time I wanted to be prepared.

"Ready," I said when I had finished packing and walked back out into the living room.

"Great. It's your turn to pick the movie by the way."

"Oh geez. Really? I have no clue what to watch."

"Well I could choose something," he said and pulled me into a hug.

I wrapped my arms around him and inhaled. His woody scent was a comfort to me now. I felt safe in his arms. Our time together was growing more serious. We watched movies, but there was a mutual tension between us. We both wanted to take things to the next level, but I could feel his hesitation, even in something as innocent as a hug.

"Come on, I'm hungry," I said breaking our connection.

I started to walk towards the door, but Josh grabbed my hand and pulled me back to him. He wrapped my arm around his waist and placed his hand on the side of my face. He looked at me then like he never had before. His expression was a mix of desire, hope and a little bit of sadness. It was dangerous.

"I want to be close to you tonight," he whispered before he kissed me.

It wasn't a soft kiss either. His mouth crashed on to mine. His hand gripped my neck as his tongue forced its way into my mouth.

I parted my lips for him and met his tongue with mine. I took a step closer to him.

"I want to be close to you too," I said between kisses.

Josh let go of my mouth and pressed his forehead to mine. He had left me breathless. Not fair. He looked into my eyes and smiled.

"What are you doing to me, Jenna?" he asked out of nowhere.

"Probably the same thing you're doing to me. I can't seem to get enough of you. I think about you all the time. Us together." I was embarrassed by my admission, but I didn't care. I was too out of breath from his kiss.

"I can't keep my hands off you. I just want to touch you all the time. Your mouth is intoxicating. I need it."

Oh. My. God. How was I supposed to respond to that? I mean, I felt the same way, but I couldn't let him know that. Not really. I was leaving at the end of the summer and I couldn't let myself get too close to him. We'd both end up hurt in the end.

"Me too," I said, despite my internal conflict.

Josh smiled again and kissed me. I let him. I needed him too. He was all I had right now. I thought of Andrew and Stefanie back in Brookhaven. I'd all but ignored them for the past month.

"Let's get back for real now. I really am hungry," I said.

"Okay," he said.

He picked up my bag and walked out of the house. I followed and locked the door on my way out.

I stopped in the middle of the sidewalk and gazed up at the sky. The sun was setting now, casting a red glow across the sky. It made me think of the old saying "red sky at night, shepherd's delight, red sky in the morning shepherd's take warning". I guess we weren't getting storms any time soon. The air was thick with humidity. It really needed to rain. I was over this sticky, sweaty feeling.

I hopped up into Josh's truck and turned the keys he'd left in the ignition. Cool air blasted against my hot skin. Thank God. The short walk from the house almost had me soaked through my thin shirt. Josh climbed into the driver's seat and threw the gears into drive and took off down the street back to his house.

CHAPTER THIRTEEN

Dinner was a delicious mix of spaghetti squash baked with garlic and olive oil and a fresh garden salad with mandarin oranges and strawberries. It was the perfect summer meal. I ate quickly then had to wait patiently for Josh to finish so we could eat the apple pie. I swear he took his sweet time just to make me wait. Even Mrs. Riley hurried him along. Finally he finished and the pie was served a la mode. Josh was right in his distinction. His mother's pie was the best in the state. It was surely the best I'd ever tasted.

"This pie is amazing," I said after my last bite.

"Thank you dear," she beamed.

I got up to help clear the plates but Josh beat me too it.

"Mom, I'll finish the dishes; Jenna, go pick out a movie."

"Don't stay up all night Josh. You have to work tomorrow."

"I know, mom!" He sounded embarrassed; I laughed awkwardly.

I was suddenly jealous of the way Josh and his mom interacted. She loved him and always felt the need to protect him from even the smallest acts. All I'd ever wanted was for my own mother to care for me and tell me that she loved me.

"I'll pull the couch out and get the bedding," she smiled at me as she left the kitchen. I forced a smile back, not because I didn't want to, but because I was trying not to let my emotions get the better of me.

"Where are the movies?" I asked Josh, mentally changing the subject.

"Down in my room," he said as he filled the sink with soapy water.

"In your bedroom?" I asked. I stood as close to him as I could without touching him.

Josh's hands gripped the sink so I knew my proximity was getting to him.

"Yes, in my room," he said.

"Okay then."

I turned and headed to the stairs that led to the basement. It was extra dark down here today. The dark blue plaid curtains covered the small daylight windows that matched the comforter and pillow shams on his queen sized bed. A dresser stood neatly in the corner and a small desk that held his laptop and printer was next to it.

Soft music was playing from somewhere. I recognized it, but it was too quiet for me to place it. I wandered over to the desk with the laptop and brushed my fingers over the touchpad. The screen lit up and showed that iTunes was open and running. I scanned the list of songs, mostly classic rock until I came to the one with the tiny speaker icon beside it. It was *Kansas*, *Carry on My Wayward Son*. One of my favorites. One year, at the River Festival in the city, a *Kansas* tribute band played and a bunch of us made the trip out there to see them. I clicked the volume button until I could hear it and restarted the song.

I looked around, but didn't immediately see a rack of DVD's. Josh was a relatively clean person, but I bet Mrs. Riley whipped through while we were gone at my house. I looked again and finally found a low shelf against the wall next to his bed. I walked around the end of his bed and sat on it and leaned low to read the titles he had. More car and action movies. I guess anything would be okay at this point. I'm not sure I'd be able to concentrate on the movie anyway. I'd be too busy keeping myself from making out with him and worrying about his mom interrupting us.

I heard a motorcycle revving and realized it was the beginning of a *Meatloaf* song. Soon the piano started. I smiled. This song reminded me of my dad. When I was like, twelve, I spent a couple weeks with him during the summer while Linda and their kids visited relatives. We didn't do anything the entire time I was there. He basically used the time away from Linda as bachelor time. He drank beer and listened to his stereo loudly all day and night.

I concentrated again on the movies. None of them sounded interesting. Before I knew it, my mind was wandering again. I felt the bed dip next to me. I looked over to see Josh sitting next to me. I smiled at him. He smiled back. He'd caught me day dreaming and he knew it. He laughed at me after a short smiling contest.

"Did you decide on something?" he asked.

"No. I'm not really into compelling action movies, especially right before bed. I tend to not sleep well."

"I see."

He got up off the bed and shut the computer. "I didn't realize I'd left the music going."

"I liked it. *Kansas* was playing when I came down."

"Ah, *Kansas*." I guessed that he was remembering the River Festival.

I got up off the bed and walked over to him.

"I don't really want to watch a movie," I admitted.

"I don't either," he said in a low voice. He turned to face me and placed his hand at his favorite spot on my body, the side of my face.

He ran his thumb over my cheek under my eye.

"What do you want to do then?" I asked breathlessly. I could feel the heat rolling off his body. It was hotter in here than it was outside. My skin was sensitive to the touch and everywhere Josh touched me sent electric pulses pinging through every fiber of my being. Josh shifted us so that his bed was behind me. He walked me backwards until the back of my knees hit the mattress.

"This," he whispered.

His low husky voice shivered through my body. I was barely aware of the fact that he was pushing me down onto the bed. When my head hit the pillow, Josh ran his fingers through my hair and placed his hands on either side of my head. He hovered over me, straddling me. I had one knee up between his legs. I knocked it against his behind so that he fell onto me. I wrapped my arms around his neck and pulled his mouth to mine. I wanted this too. So unbelievably bad. Our weeks of making out on my ugly couch had left me wanting to do more with him than I had with anyone else.

His hands were in my hair again. I grabbed his shirt in my hands and pulled it over his head. His tanned chest now bare above me. I pulled my hands from his back and pressed them into his chest then ran them over his broad shoulders. I felt one of his hands at my hip. He reached up under my shirt and skimmed over my stomach. I sucked in and exhaled all at the same time. My skin was on fire now, his touch igniting it. I slipped my hands down to his belt. I fiddled with it but he stopped me.

"My mom is still awake," he said.

I dropped my head and hands to the bed. Cold water had been poured over me at the mention of Mrs. Riley. I felt guilty. She'd opened up to me today and allowed me to stay in her home because she cared about my safety and here I was violating her trust. I sat up and pushed Josh off of me.

"I'm sorry," he said.

"Don't be. It's customary now for you to get me all hot and bothered, then stop and leave me wanting you."

"Hey, that's not fair," he said while putting his shirt back on.

"Whatever," I said. I leaned over the side of his bed and grabbed the first movie my hand found. I threw it at him. "Here, we can watch this." I rolled off the bed and walked out of his room and up the stairs without looking at him.

It's not like I was really expecting us to have sex tonight or anything, but it would be nice to be satisfied at least once instead of him getting me all worked up for nothing. Ugh! I was over thinking this again.

When I got to the living room, one side table lamp had been turned on as well as the television. The hide-a-bed had been pulled out for me and bright yellow sheets with gigantic sunflowers printed on them covered the thin mattress. Two pillows were propped up against the back of the couch each with a sunflower printed off center on the cases. I smiled at how perfect these sheets fit Mrs. Riley's personality. Yellow must be her favorite color.

"Jenna, what's going on?"

"What do you mean?" I turned to face him.

"Why'd you storm off up the stairs? Are you mad at me?"

"No, I'm just frustrated at myself."

"Why?"

The real answer to his question loomed over me like a dark cloud. I didn't want to admit to him that I was falling for him. I didn't want to admit it to myself. I reminded myself that I was leaving at the end of the summer so I couldn't be attached to anything. Not Josh, not the house, nothing.

"I don't know."

"No. You can't answer with that anymore." He was mad now. "Say what you want to say, Jenna."

"Josh, I can't let myself fall for you. I'm leaving at the end of the summer and I probably won't be coming back again. Ever." There, I said it. I spit it out. I couldn't even look at him.

I stood there in the semi-darkness with my arms hung down at my sides and stared down at the carpet. I felt Josh move in front of me. He put one arm around my waist and the other on the back of my neck. He drew me into him. I stumbled and caught myself on his hips. My face was pressed into the space between his shoulder and neck. I lifted my arms up and hooked them on the back of his shoulders.

"Jenna, I'm falling for you," he said into the air. "I think I love you."

I smiled into his shoulder. Most girls would be upset by, 'I think' and that he didn't look into my eyes when he said those three words. But I wasn't most girls. I hadn't grown up hearing, 'I love you'. My dad said it when he talked to me, but it was hurried and hushed over the phone. I knew this would end eventually, but for now, for tonight, I was grateful for Josh's presence. A single tear escaped my eyes and I pressed it into his shirt.

"I think I love you too," I returned.

We kissed again in the living room. I wished I hadn't stormed up the stairs. Our admission of 'I love you' could have been downstairs and I could have kissed him more passionately without the worry of his mom walking in.

We decided not to watch the movie; instead, we kissed not so briefly again and then went to bed. I fell asleep as soon as my head hit the pillow, I didn't even realize how tired I was.

***

The next morning, I woke up to the sound of bacon sizzling. I loved bacon, bacon was the reason I could never be a vegetarian. I scrambled out of bed and changed into shorts and a t-shirt in the bathroom and wandered into the kitchen.

"Good morning, Mrs. Riley," I said. Her back was to me and she turned at the sound of my voice

"Good morning, Jenna. Did you sleep well? You looked like you did."

"Yeah, I didn't realize how tired I was."

"Would you like some breakfast?"

I grabbed some plates from the cabinet next to her and set the table for three. I pulled out some silverware and napkins too and placed them around the table. I sat at the table and watched her as she finished the breakfast prep. I realized then that Mrs. Riley was always baking or cooking when I came over. What did she do all day when Josh was at school and work? Did she work? I thought back to when we were in middle and high school, but I couldn't think of her ever having a job or working outside the home.

"Do you have a job, Mrs. Riley?" I blurted out my thoughts before I could stop myself. I usually had a good filter for this kind of thing.

"No honey," she said as she spooned out eggs and bacon onto my plate. "Josh's dad pays alimony and we had a large settlement after the divorce. Josh and I don't need much, so what we have is enough to live on."

"I see." I wasn't sure what to say after that.

I ate most of my breakfast in silence, wondering when Josh would be awake and join us. Even though Mrs. Riley and I had come to an understanding and let go of things that had happened in the past, I still felt awkward around her. I didn't like being alone with her because I felt like I had to carry on a conversation with her, but I didn't know what to say. The only things we had in common were Josh and the fact that my mom was the cause of her divorce and that wasn't a subject I wanted to expand on.

"What are you studying in school Jenna?" she asked breaking the silence.

"Psychology," I said between bites of bacon.

"Oh, that's interesting. Why did you choose that?"

"It goes back to my childhood. I feel like I've had to deal with a lot and I'm barely eighteen. I want to help other girls, well, children in general, who have difficult home-lives overcome their challenges and realize that there is more to life than what they've been given. Drug and alcohol abuse are not the norm. These kids have potential; they just need someone to believe in them and get to the root of the issue, and fix that instead of just trying to fix the kid. I know there are agencies and programs that cater to these kids, but sometimes I feel like they are built on old-fashioned principles and standards. Kids these days are different, and we need to restructure the way we as adults and professionals reach out to them to help them. My dream is to start a new program to help kids realize their potential and get them resources to get out of the life they are in."

"That's quite a dream you have."

"For now it's just a dream. I need to finish school first."

"Do you not think you will?" A look of concern crossed her face.

I leaned back in my chair and pushed my empty plate to the center of the table. I knew I would finish school, but what I didn't know was if I had to motivation to further my education to do what I wanted to do.

"I'll finish school, but to do anything in psychology you have to have a Master's degree. That's a lot of time and school and I just don't know if I want to keep going."

"Why?" Mrs. Riley seemed genuinely interested in me and my plans for the future.

"I don't know. I think that's part of the reason I came back to Riverview for the summer, to gain a little perspective and maybe find some closure for what happened when I left.

"Closure?"

"When my mom was sent to jail, I had no one on my side. I was three months from eighteen. Three months from being out on my own. If they'd just let me go, who knows what would have happened. I wouldn't have gone to my dad's but I also felt like I was being treated like a child. I wasn't given a choice, I was just shuttled off to his house because I wasn't legally an adult. I still don't know all the details of my situation, but if I'd had some kind of advocate or even just a safe place to go when everything went down, better decisions could have been made. I could have finished school here with Josh and Michelle. I could have made my own decisions about my future."

"But I thought you liked your dad."

"I do. I'm glad I was sent to him, but I think about all the other kids who don't have a stable parent, who are just shuttled around until they age out of the system. The thing I didn't like was that I wasn't given an option. It was go to my dad's or go to foster care. And then my dad and Linda had to have a home inspection and all that stuff and Linda was just livid about the whole thing. Dad later told me that if we'd been able to talk about it, he would have signed the papers for me to be an emancipated minor and I could have just stayed here and finished school. It would have saved a little heartache on both sides."

"I see," Mrs. Riley said. "So you wanted to stay here. Do you want to stay here now?"

"I just wanted to finish school here. I felt like everything just got so crazy and I didn't get to say goodbye to anyone, especially Michelle and Josh." I noticed Mrs. Riley fidgeted in her seat and looked down at her lap at the mention of Michelle.

"Where is Michelle?" I asked.

"You'll have to talk to Josh about that," she said looking at me again.

"Well I have and he won't tell me anything. Did something happen between them?"

"Jenna, I…" She trailed off and looked past me. I knew Josh was there.

"Hey you two," his slow drawl sent shivers down my spine. He didn't even say anything sexy and my body was ready for anything he would do to me. "What are you talking about?" He took a seat between his mom and me and helped himself to the bacon and eggs in the middle of the table.

"Jenna was just telling me about her school and her plans for the future." Mrs. Riley said with a smile.

"Oh yeah. What are you going to do?"

"I'm not sure yet. Nothing has been decided" I looked down at the red checkered tablecloth.

Josh and I spent the rest of the morning cleaning up the

kitchen for Mrs. Riley, then he had to go off to work. He said I should stay, but I felt awkward just sitting around his house. Like, what was I supposed to do all day? After Josh left, I packed up my things, put the hideaway bed back together, and waited for Mrs. Riley to reappear. She'd gone back to her room while Josh and I cleaned up.

Finally, after about forty-five minutes and countless thoughts of just leaving, she emerged from the back rooms into the living room.

"I'm going to head out." I said before she'd even made into the room.

"Oh, alright," her face fell a little at my words.

"I just want to check in at home and call my dad."

"Have you told him what's going on?"

"No. It would only worry him and he's got a family to worry about."

"You're his family too," she said sternly.

"I know."

After a short pause, she said, "Okay, well you are welcome to come back and stay. I know I was hesitant before about you staying here, but I was wrong. This is a serious situation and I don't want you to get hurt."

The sentiment behind her words was real. She cared about me like my own mother didn't. She cared about her son's girlfriend, someone who wasn't even related to her, someone who was connected with her marriage ending, and someone with whom she had no business caring about, but she did. My heart swelled and tears formed behind my eyes. The stark difference between her and my own mother hit me like a ton of bricks. This was the reason I was in school and the reason I needed to continue. I needed to be the one to care for a child the way Mrs. Riley cared for me. I needed kids in my situation to know that they mattered to someone.

I got up off the couch, walked over to her, and hugged her. She immediately embraced me putting one hand around my back and one on my head.

"Oh Sweetheart" was all she had to say and the tears that

threatened were now spilling over my eyelashes and down my cheeks. I cried quickly and silently, wiping my face when I pulled away from her.

"Thank you Mrs. Riley. I'll be back later." I left quickly, leaving her watching me go in the living room.

I spent the next few nights with Josh and his mom. She cooked amazing dinners like enchiladas, chicken and rice casserole, and lasagna, which was way better than my frozen meal by far. Mrs. Riley let me stay downstairs with Josh in his room to watch TV and hangout, but when it was time for bed, I always came upstairs and slept on the pullout bed even though Josh protested each night. But I just couldn't disrespect her kindness like that. During the day Mrs. Riley and I talked about the situation with my mom and tried to think of who else might be in on the whole thing. We knew the mayor and the sweaty man who came to my house that day, but since neither of us know who that man was, there could potentially be other people involved that we didn't even know about.

CHAPTER FOURTEEN

"Jenna. Fancy meeting you here," the mayor said with a sneer.

I was about to find a new grocery store. I had decided to buy a few items to help restock Mrs. Riley after staying at her house for the past week. It was the least I could do.

This was the second time I'd run into him and it was two times too many. I didn't even want to respond to him. Not now that I knew he was behind the attack in my own home. I wasn't even going to bother to finish my shopping. So I abandoned my cart and walked the other way.

"Don't you turn your back on me." He hurried over to me, grabbed the back of my t-shirt, and held me against him. "I know you've been staying with the Riley's. You don't want them involved in this mess. Yes, I know you know what I'm talking about. You better find what you have of mine and return it to me."

"I don't have anything of yours. Let me go." I struggled against him, but he held on to me.

"Don't play games Jenna." I frantically looked around the store in hopes that someone would pass by and see us, but no one did.

"I'll call the police," I said. It didn't come out as threatening as I wanted it to.

"And tell them what? That your mother was still trafficking drugs through your house even though she's in jail. That you came back to help her? That you are using that poor innocent Riley boy to do your business for you? Face it Jenna, I have you cornered. Get me what's mine, and no one will get hurt."

He pushed me and let me go. I didn't turn to look at him. I headed straight for the door at a run and hightailed it out of the parking lot as fast as my car would take me. I texted Josh.

Meet me now. You know where.

***

I waited for Josh for the better part of an hour before giving up. I stripped down to my suit and slipped into the river. The water bubbled happily over my feet, sending chills up my spine despite the fact that it was over a hundred degrees today.

"Watch out for snakes," came Josh's low rumble of a voice. I smiled, my back was to him, but I knew he was staring at me.

"Thanks for the warning."

I heard his sandals flop as he walked down the embankment to the water. I didn't turn around to face him, but let him walk up beside me and stand, both of us staring out over the clear water. I side glanced at him. He was wearing bright orange board shorts and a blue t-shirt with *Dodgers* printed across it. Memories flooded the forefront of my mind. He always wore that shirt to the river. In high school we'd party down here. The girls would be in the water or lounging on the banks while the boys played a pickup game of soccer. Even after he and I broke up, I'd still catch myself watching him. I even watched him kiss Michelle and wish it was me.

I let out a breath of air and moved further into the water. The slimy moss covered rocks squished between my toes. Josh rustled beside me. I guessed that he was removing his shoes and shirt. I kept going. At its deepest, the river was to my neck. I walked until it covered my hips. I lifted my arms and skimmed the water with my fingertips creating tiny waves all around me. Josh came up behind me. He stood unusually close to me, the warmth of his body sizzling against my back.

"Jenna." He breathed in my ear sending shivers of desire down my spine. My heart rate accelerated, deep breaths heaved in my chest. What was he doing to me? All he did was say my name. I leaned back slightly so my back was touching his chest. I leaned my head back against his shoulder. He met me with a soft kiss on my temple. I reached up and ran my fingers down his arms to his hands. I took them in mine and pulled them around me. I placed them on my stomach and reached one hand up and around his neck. He kissed my temple again, then trailed tiny kisses down to my ear, then down my neck. I gasped and drew in a deep breath. That must have been enough for him because he spun me around to face him.

I was met with his glistening, tanned, well-toned chest. I

couldn't stop staring at it. I watched it rise and fall with each breath he took. I attempted to match my breathing to his in hopes it would calm me, but his breathing was just as erratic as mine. I tentatively reached up and put my hand on his chest over his heart. It was racing just like mine. He flinched at my touch so I pulled away and we just stood there, inches apart, breathing each other's air as the river rushed passed us.

I had no idea what Josh was thinking right now, but I wanted to know. I wanted to ask him why he was still here in this going-no-where town, why he wasn't with Michelle anymore and why was he here with me now.

Before I could get my words out, his right hand was cupping my face. He tilted my head up to meet his so I was gazing into his stormy blue eyes. He searched my eyes with his before lowering his gaze to my mouth. I parted my lips and drew in a breath. I barely had time to exhale before his lips were on mine. This wasn't a soft, test the waters, kind of kiss. His hand was pressed to my face, his left hand squeezed just above my hip then snaked around and rested on my lower back. The current of the river nudged me so I fell into him. My hands gripped his waist.

I pulled him to me and returned his kiss. I parted my lips and granted his tongue access to mine. Both of his hands were in my hair now as his tongue danced with mine. I slid my hands up his back, gripping his firm muscles along the way. A soft groan escaped from his throat, igniting an old flame I thought I'd long extinguished.

Josh pushed me gently backwards so I was heading into deeper water. He pulled away from our kiss, but only briefly. He continued pressing his mouth to mine, mirroring the soft flowing current of the river. Before I knew it, he was trailing kisses under my chin and down my neck. I was now chest deep in the water and my feet were slipping on the rocks at the bottom. Josh released my head and held me around my waist, pressing my hips to his.

I gasped at his erection pressing against me. This only spurred him on. He pulled at the strings that tied my suit top on until it fell away freeing, my breasts. His left hand traveled up the side of my body until he cupped me and massaged gently, his right hand still holding me to him. I stopped kissing him and looked him square in the eyes. Longing flashed over his face, probably mirroring my own expression. I bit my bottom lip between my teeth and slipped my hand beneath the waistband of his shorts and took hold of him, sliding my hands up and down his hard shaft. He looked hungrily down at me and kissed me hard again.

He groaned in protest when I released him, but I quickly hopped up and wrapped my legs around his waist and squeezed against him. I felt him smile against my lips and I smiled back at him and kissed him again.

He started walking toward the opposite side of the river. With his long strides, it didn't take long. I knew where we were. The shadow of the massive willow tree engulfed us and soon my back was pressed up against its smooth trunk. The water stayed deep where he walked, so it almost covered my shoulders.

Josh started kissing me again, but now that I was wedged against the tree, his hands were free to roam my body. And roam they did. He started at my breasts and cupped and squeezed them both. He then moved down slowly, taking in every inch of me then grabbing my ass. He untied each side of the bottoms of my suit until it fell away. *I need a new suit,* I thought to myself. All thoughts were quickly erased when Josh slid his hand over my thighs and between my legs. I let out a soft moan causing Josh to kiss me harder and pull me down against his ready and waiting member.

I pushed him away from me and tried to pull his shorts off, but they stuck to him. We both struggled until finally they fell away. Josh pushed me up against the tree trunk again and simultaneously pulled me down so he entered me full on. I cried out his name and clung to his neck, but he pushed me up, guiding my hands above my head.

"Hold on to the tree," he whispered. I did what he said and grasped the tree with both hands. He stood firm against the bottom of the river, placed both hands on either side of my hips, and began to thrust into me. The cool water lapped against my skin, igniting my senses. I could feel each thrust, the sound of the water in time with them cut through the silence around us. I threw my head back allowing Josh access to my neck. He took it and trailed kisses down to my collarbone, gently sucking at my tender skin. I moaned again and Josh pumped harder against me. I gripped the tree as I felt my body building toward its release until I came hard around him. I let go and wrapped my arms around him. He still pounded into me so I kissed his neck up to his ear and licked it. I felt his body tense and he pulled my hips against his and held me there. I felt his own release inside me. He let me go and we floated out into the water.

I found footing and stopped myself. Josh did the same and walked over to me. He took my face in both of his hands and locked his blue eyes onto my hazel.

"That was amazing." And he kissed me.

It was amazing and completely unexpected. I wasn't sure what to think about what we'd just done. I mean, I wasn't a virgin, I'd had a short fling with a guy at school. But it was nothing compared to what I'd just experienced with Josh.

"Are you okay?" he asked.

I just nodded. I was still processing everything. We'd just had sex in the river. Against a willow tree. All I wanted was to lie next to him and for him to hold me. But we were in a river. Naked. Oh god. I looked around but our respective swim suits were missing. I knew I had shorts and a t-shirt on the bank I could wear, Josh on the other hand, had showed up in his trunks and the Dodger shirt.

"Do you have pants?" I blurted. After all of that, I was worried about him having pants?

Josh laughed.

"I do. I have a pair of old jeans in the truck."

"Okay."

"Is that what you're thinking about right now? My pants?"

He still held my face loosely in his hands so I leaned into his palms as I laughed.

"Yeah, I guess."

"Come on. Let's get dry."

We waded out of the river. I stayed back and watched the evening sun bounce off the glistening water that rolled off his backside. Damn, he had a nice ass.

"Here." He threw his towel at me. I wrapped it around myself and walked up to his truck. I gathered the clothes I'd folded on the ground and slipped into my shorts and tank top. I looked up at Josh to find him staring at me.

I blushed as he watched me get dressed. I was just glad I didn't do the hopping on one leg thing I usually did when I would get dressed.

"Hey," I said.

"Hey," he replied.

I walked up to his truck and into his arms.

"What are you doing to me?" I asked into his neck.

"Me? It's you who is doing the things."

"That doesn't even make sense." I kissed his neck again.

"Keep doing that and I'll be ready for round two," he said.

It was a hot day, but cold heat exploded through my body. Just the thought of having Josh again was enough to make me shiver with desire. I looked him in the eyes, searching them. All I saw as intensity.

I almost kissed him again, but before I could, he leaned in and whispered something in my ear. Something I'd rarely heard and never sincerely experienced.

"I love you."

I stilled. Frozen. He'd said those words again, this time with no 'I think' before them. Walls I didn't know I'd built crashed around me. I held on to Josh. I pulled him against me in a fierce embrace. Tears spilled over my cheeks but I doubted he would notice because we were both still wet from the river.

No one had ever said those words to me like that before. I don't ever remember hearing them from my mom, and my dad whispered them hurriedly when Linda wasn't around. Josh said them loud and to me, to my heart. Granted, we were alone at the moment, but I have no doubt he'd proclaim his love for me publicly if given the chance.

"I love you too, Josh," I said.

I meant it. I did love him. We'd been friends for years, but it was more than that now. I felt safe with Josh. He made me feel wanted and beautiful, two things no one had ever made me feel before. No one except Andrew. I sighed heavily in Josh's arms.

"What is it?" he asked.

"Nothing," I said quickly. How could I explain Andrew to Josh? How was I going to explain Josh to Andrew? I had been friends with Josh for years, so we just made sense together. We could figure out the logistics of our relationship later. Right now, I wasn't worried about leaving at the end of the summer. Right now, all I cared about was the two of us together and what we had just done in the river.

Josh's arms tightened around me so I squeezed him a little tighter as well. I didn't want to move, I wanted to stay in this moment forever.

"I'm assuming you didn't tell me to meet you here so we could do that?" he asked, breaking the magicalness of the moment.

"No, not really."

Josh laughed at me then.

"It was good. Don't get me wrong. The best I've ever had."

"Wait, you're not a virgin?"

"Josh. Seriously. That's not why I need to talk to you either."

"I'm just messing with you. I'm not either."

I did a double take at his last comment, but chose to ignore it in light of what I really needed to tell him.

"What is it?" he asked.

"I ran into the mayor again. He was forceful with me and threatened me."

"Did he touch you?" Josh grabbed my arm and looked me over. His eyes had grown dark and anger played across his face.

"Yes." I looked down at my bare feet. "He grabbed the back of my shirt and held me against him while he threatened me."

He lifted my chin so I had to look at his face.

"What did he say?" His voice was flat and hard. He was serious.

"He said that I needed to hand over the drugs or someone would get hurt. Actually, he said 'Get me what's mine and no one will get hurt.'" I sighed before continuing. "He said that I couldn't really call the police because no one would believe me."

It was Josh's turn to sigh. "He's probably right. We have no proof of his involvement in any of this."

"I know."

CHAPTER FIFTEEN

Josh and I were sitting on the couch staring mindlessly at the TV. I'd had the bright idea to introduce him to the *Lord of the Rings*, but neither of us had the mindset to actually pay attention to the movie. We both knew why he was here. Ever since our 'river event' as I liked to think of it, we haven't been able to hang out like we used to. Last night I tried just watching a TV show but I was so distracted by, well, everything about him, I didn't remember what we watched. We ended up making out on the couch for two hours.

The next night was the same way. We were in our usual position, I seated at one end of the couch with his head in my lap, and his body stretched out over the length of the couch. Josh wasn't watching the movie at all. He was either staring intently at me, distracting me, or his eyes were closed like he was trying to think of what to say or do to me next. I was about to shut off the movie and say something to him, but he beat me too it.

"Jenna," Josh said.

"Yeah," I whispered back. I'm not sure why I whispered.

"What are we doing?"

"Watching a movie?" I offered.

"No, I mean us. What are we doing?"

"Spending time together?" Every answer came out like a question.

"What else?"

"What do you mean?"

"Where are we going?"

I had been waiting for this conversation. I hadn't kept my feelings about staying here long term a secret. He knew I was going to leave at the end of the summer. But neither of us had denied strong feelings for each other, and our admission of love had me questioning everything at this point.

"You tell me."

"Well, you're leaving at the end of the summer and might not be coming back."

I thought about this. He was right. I wasn't sure what my plans were for next summer. What if I had a job, or needed to take summer classes? What if my mom got out of jail?

"I don't really have any plans. I could come back. It depends on a lot of things."

Josh popped up off my lap, leaving my hands empty. His hair was slicked to one side where I'd brushed it back and stuck out at odd ends on the other side where his head had been against my lap.

"Jenna, I'm in love with you. I want you for more than the summer. Can't you give me that?"

"Like quit school?"

"No, I would never ask that of you. But would you move here if I waited for you?"

Words left me. My mouth hung open and my eyes went blank. Josh had just told me he'd wait for me. Weren't girls supposed to be the ones to go all gooey eyed and wait for their man to make a decision? I just didn't know what to say.

"Um, I don't know Josh. That's a huge step to think about," I said, finally.

"Why?" he asked.

"I want to finish school. And you know my history with this town. I don't want to live here,"

"Where do you want to live?"

"I hadn't really thought about that," I said.

"Then think about here,"

"Why can't you think about living somewhere else?" I asked after a brief pause.

"I can't leave my mom here alone," he scoffed

"She's a grown woman; I think she'll be fine."

"We're all each other has."

"I don't want to live here for the rest of my life, Josh."

I'd all but made up my mind. Small town living wasn't for me. I wasn't one to sit at home all day while my husband worked the fields. I wanted to be a guidance counselor in a school, and with only one school system in this area, there wasn't much of a place for me.

We sat in silence for a while. I wasn't sure if we were done talking and if I could resume watching the movie. Josh had to be lost since we hadn't been paying much attention to it.

"What if I came with you after the summer was over?" he said.

"What about your mom?" I questioned.

"I don't know. I never thought I could leave her, but now I'm thinking about it."

"What about your job?"

Josh sat up quickly and stared at me. His mouth was set in a hard line.

"You are making a lot of excuses as to why we shouldn't be together in the future, Jenna."

He was right, but I didn't want to be stuck in a town where no one liked me and where I wasn't wanted. I didn't want to take him away from his mom either. I didn't know what to say, so I just stared back at him and kept my thoughts to myself.

"Why are you staring at me?" Josh asked, interrupting my thoughts.

"Umm…" My phone rang at that moment. Really? I glanced at the caller ID. If Andrew ever had perfect timing, it was now. I ignored it. It wasn't a good time.

"Who was that?" Josh asked. He looked at me sideways like he knew who was calling me.

"No one," I lied.

"Boyfriend from college?" This was the first time Andrew had called while I was with Josh. Josh and I hadn't even talked about the possibility of me having a relationship in Brookhaven. Actually, we hadn't even talked about Brookhaven at all until now.

I looked down at the phone in my hands, not saying anything. I heard Josh sigh and shift on the couch away from me.

"So you have a boyfriend?" I really didn't want to answer this. So I leaned over to him and kissed him instead.

"There are way funner things we could be doing with our mouths than talking," I said between kisses.

"Is funner a word?"

"Stop talking," I said and pushed him on the couch. "This

couch needs more action, it's ugly,"

I straddled Josh's lap and allowed him to remove my shirt. I took his off too. We stared at each other for a moment but before my conscious mind could take over, he devoured me with a kiss. Josh's hands traveled up my back and unhooked my bra strap. Andrew was all but forgotten until my phone rang again.

"Do you need to get that?" Josh said. He was irritated. He gently pushed me off of his lap and back onto the couch.

"Um, no. No I don't."

I turned my phone to vibrate and threw in on the floor, but it immediately started ringing again.

"Seriously just answer your phone."

I snatched it up off the floor where it had fallen.

"It stopped." It started again. Damn it. Josh just looks at me and waved his hand at me.

"Hello?" I said a little exasperated.

"Jenna! What are you doing?" It was Andrew, he always seemed to call at inopportune moments. Like right now, while I was making out with Josh.

"I'm just hanging out, watching a movie," I laughed nervously.

"That's it?" He sounded like he didn't believe me.

"Um, yeah. There isn't much to do in this town,"

"I see," he sounded as though he didn't believe me.

"What are you doing?" I asked.

"Working."

"That's it?" I countered.

Andrew laughed. He had a great laugh. It was deep and smooth like the roll of a drum. The kind of laugh that when you heard it, you just couldn't help but laugh along, or at least smile. "Yes Jen, that's all. Summer is boring and you're the only girl I have eyes for if that's what you're hinting at."

"That's not it at all." I think my voice rose a couple of octaves, I hoped not because that would give everything away.

I didn't know why I had been ignoring Andrew's phone calls all summer. He really did call at bad times, and I felt weird talking to him in front of Josh.

"Okay," he said after a beat "well I was worried some studly farm boy had stolen your heart." I glanced over at Josh with that comment. Had Josh stolen my heart?

Nervous laughter again.

"Yeah, well I have to go, it's late. I'll call you later," I said too quickly.

"But wait, we just started talking." I could tell he was getting a little suspicious.

"Yeah well, I'm just busy."

"Busy doing what?"

"Watching a movie?" I obviously wasn't busy. "Haven't we already established that?"

I looked at Josh again and he had his arms folded across his chest, his eyes squinted at me questioningly. I looked away from him and down at my feet.

"I see."

"Yeah."

"Yeah," he repeated.

"Well, have a good rest of the summer," I said.

"Yeah, you too," he said and with that, I hung up.

I dropped my arms to my side and released the breath I didn't even know I was holding. I turned back to Josh; he sat upright on the couch with his arms folded and raised his eyebrows at me. We just stared at each other for a moment

"I should go," he said finally and made to get up off the couch.

"Wait, you don't have to leave." I rushed over to him and pushed him back on the couch and sat next to him. "Don't go."

"Who was that on the phone?" he asked like he was accusing me of some heinous crime.

I sighed. I had done a lot of sighing.

"It's no one you need to worry about." I wasn't sure I wanted to divulge into who Andrew was and what he meant to me.

"Okay," he said simply, but he looked past me and squared his jaw. I wanted to know what he was thinking.

Josh stood up from the couch and threw his shirt back on. He walked past me to the door handing me mine along the way. I followed him.

"Where are you going?" I thought we had established that I wanted him to stay.

"The phone call was kind of a mood killer. I should just go. I have to work tomorrow anyway."

"Josh," I whined.

"Jenna, I made my feelings for you clear the other day at the river, and I thought you did too, but now I'm not so sure. You need to figure things out."

"Okay. Yeah." I did nothing to hide my disappointment.

"I'll see you tomorrow though, okay?" he said and leaned in to kiss my cheek.

"For what?"

"I don't know." He whispered in my ear when he hugged me. I smiled.

"I love you," I said before I kissed him long and slow so he had to hold my face and wrap his arm around me. Mixed feelings raced through my mind. I'd fallen for Josh, hard, but there was Andrew. I needed to figure out what was going to happen between us when I went back to school.

A small knock on the screen door startled both of us. Lauren stood on my porch bathed in the dim yellow light of the porch light holding a casserole dish.

"Hi Lauren." My voice came out several octaves above my normal range.

"Lauren," Josh said coolly and opened the door for her. What the hell was he doing? I didn't want her in here, especially after we'd just almost had sex on the couch.

"I…uh…my mom made you this because she was worried you were eating only peanut butter and jelly. I told her you did not have a lot of food in the house after I stayed at your here, so she made a lasagna and some kind of beef casserole. I just wanted to drop it off," she said quickly, not looking at either of us.

"Thanks, Lauren," I said and grabbed the two dishes from her.

"You're welcome," she said, still not looking at me.

The silence was deafeningly awkward. We all shifted from one foot to the other and back again.

"Well I should go," Josh said finally, his voice was really loud and obnoxious. He left quickly without another word and all but sprinted to his truck. The tires squealed as he sped away. Geez.

"So you and Josh," Lauren squeaked.

"Yeah," I said sheepishly.

"I wonder what Michelle would think."

"I don't know. I haven't seen her."

"You haven't?" Lauren looked appalled.

"No," I looked away from her. Her reaction bothered me. I looked back at Lauren again. She had her lips pursed together like she really wanted to say something but was debating whether or not to tell me. Knowing Lauren, this was an extremely difficult feat.

"What is it, Lauren?" I coaxed. I was usually good at getting things out of people.

At the sound of my voice, she snapped out of her internal dilemma and stalked to the door.

"You'll just have to ask Josh about this one." And she left without another word. I'm sure her tires would have squealed too if she'd been a less cautious driver.

Two people had left my house in an uncomfortable rush and I was left here alone and confused. Why did it even matter what Michelle thought? She had to know I was here. She'd made no effort to come see me. I guess I haven't gone up to see her either though. We're both bad friends. I think she should make the first move though. I didn't have any real logic behind it other than it should just be that way because it's less awkward for me.

My phone pinged at me, notifying me of a text message. It was Andrew again. I rolled my eyes before answering it.

we need to talk about what just happened

CHAPTER SIXTEEN

"Josh, everyone will know about us now!" I said exasperatedly into the phone. I'd called him almost as soon as Lauren had left. I was freaking out. I'd ignored Andrew's text and decided to deal with him another day.

"So? Why is that such a bad thing?" I could tell he was still upset by our conversation earlier.

He had a good point I guess. Why did it matter? He was the one being secretive about our relationship to begin with and now he seemed fine with it. I had wanted to have a quiet summer away from everything and it was quickly dissolving right before my eyes.

"It's not, I guess." I rolled off the couch and turned the TV on. I flipped through some channels and landed on MTV. It was sad that they didn't play music videos anymore.

"So now everyone knows we've been hanging out together."

"And kissing," I interrupted Josh.

"And probably more by now. We should go out to the bonfire Friday night at the river,"

"The bonfire?" I asked. First he was mad at me and now he was suggesting we go out. Out in public.

"For the Fourth of July," he said like I should know what he was talking about.

"It's tradition! Everyone goes."

"I'm not sure that's a good idea, Josh."

"I really want to go and I don't want to go without you."

"I have never participated in this tradition."

"Seriously? Michelle never dragged you out?" He stopped short with his words like he regretted something he said.

"No, I blew her off."

"Let's go then."

I was silent on the phone while I contemplated what to do.

"Please," he pleaded. I imagined his eyes. They probably looked sad and puppy doggish. If he were here in person, I would say yes in a heartbeat. I didn't know what it was about those stormy blues, but I just lost my head when I stared into them.

"Well if you're going to whine about it," I said.

"I'm not whining!"

"Okay okay! I'll go." I had given in too easily.

"Great!"

Josh's mood seemed to have done a one-eighty, but I wasn't going to complain. If going to the bonfire tonight was going to get his mind off the inevitable fact that I was still leaving at the end of the summer and that we needed to figure out what that meant for us, then I'd go. Besides, we'd been holed up in my house or his all summer now, the least I could do was go out with him just this once. There'd be a ton of people out there anyway, which was a good thing in a way, I would probably run into the kids I used to go to school with, but kids from the whole county came out to this bonfire, so my chances of seeing people, especially in the dark, were slim. I'd just stay with Josh and steer clear of any familiar faces.

"You know what this means, don't you?" I asked.

"No, what?" he responded.

"We'll be back at the river,"

"In the river?"

"Mmmhmmm," I said trying to be seductive.

"You'd do it in the river again?" he asked, catching my drift.

"Yes. Would you?"

"I'd go anywhere with you." My seductiveness must have worked.

"Well I'm about to hop in the shower if you want to go there with me." Yes, I was totally going there.

"I'll be right there." He hung up the phone before I could say anything else.

Little fiery butterflies ignited in my belly. The memory of us in the river and the possibility of more excited me.

Josh was at the front door in record time.

"Hey," he said slowly.

"Hey," I blushed.

"How about that shower?" he teased.

I started walking backwards and he followed. I grabbed his hand and turned, pulling him along behind me. Once in the bathroom, Josh's expression changed instantly. His eyes darkened and his face turned serious. The butterflies he ignited while we were still on the phone sprang from my belly into every inch of my body, setting every nerve on fire. I needed to get into that shower soon or I was going to explode into flames.

I slipped out of my clothes and quickly turned the water on and hopped in. I was blasted with ice-cold water, just what I needed to cool down before Josh came in. I heard him shuffle on the other side of the curtain, then waited anxiously as he slowly pulled in back.

"Hey there," he said seductively.

I just stood there at the back of the tub letting the warming water wash over my legs, my eyes glued to his body. All of it. He stepped in and dipped his head under the steady stream of water. Still unable to speak, I watched the tiny droplets of water wash over his blond hair, down over his closed eyes, and over his cheeks. At that point, some dripped off his chin to the bottom of the tub, but some slid down the side of his neck, over his tight, muscled chest, down even further over his washboard abs and past his hips. I lost the droplets there but I didn't raise my eyes back up to find a new one to follow.

"Jenna," Josh said softly.

I snapped my head up to meet his eyes. He stepped toward me out of the shower's flow. I could feel my body tense in anticipation of his touch and when it came, I instantly relaxed, falling into him and letting him hold me. He placed one hand on the side of my face, the other was wrapped around my waist. He kissed me softly on the lips then pulled away. I whimpered and threw my arms around his neck and pulled him back to me, crashing my lips against his.

"I want you," he said between kisses.

"I want you too," I returned.

He turned me and pressed my back up against the wall. We were totally going to have sex in my shower.

***

"Are you only allowed to have sex in water?" I asked playfully. I was about to blow-dry my hair. It was kind of a pointless action, seeing as we were sitting at about ninety percent humidity, but it was habit, and I wanted my hair to at least start out looking decent.

"Apparently," Josh said from behind me. "We should get going soon,"

I flipped off the blow dryer and ran a brush through my long hair one more time. I had to search for my old bathing suit since the new one I'd bought last year was somewhere down the river. I finally found it at the bottom of my closet. It still fit, but barely. My boobs were bigger than they used to be and weren't as well covered as I liked them to be. Josh didn't seem to mind. He stared at my chest the whole rest of the time I was getting ready. I finally had to grab a tank top and cover up so we could leave.

We finally left the house, but we sat in his truck in front of my house for another twenty minutes and kissed. He couldn't keep his hands off my chest and I regretted putting on the bikini. I wasn't going to swim in the river in the dark anyway. I finally pushed him off me and we set out down the road to the old high way. The sun had all but set with only a thin line of orange visible on the horizon. As I sat in his truck remembering what had just happened in the shower, and just now in the truck, the song Josh had claimed as ours, came on the radio.

"Hey, listen to that," Josh said proudly. He looked over at me with a huge grin on his face. "It's our song,"

"It's not our song," I said. I leaned my head back and just stared at the ceiling of the truck.

"If you say so," he said and continued to sing along with the song.

I just stared out the window and tried to tune out the music. I watched the houses disappear and the farmland take over. First, the cows scattered over the fields, then the crops began and carried on past the turn off for the river. There was my 'secret' way to the river, but there was actually a simpler way there. If you followed the old highway and turned down the second dirt road on the right, then drove about a mile, the road ended right at the river. Everyone backed their trucks up to the water, opened their tailgates and we'd just sit, drink, and talk it up until the fireworks from the next town over start popping up over the tree line. I'd been out here once, my freshman year, but I wasn't well received. I was asked repeatedly if I had any drugs on me and when I said no, I was called a slut or a whore. It was sad really.

This town couldn't get beyond who their parents were. It wasn't just me either. Of course, Michelle had an in because her dad was the mayor. Being the mayor of a town of less than five hundred people didn't mean much, but to this town it meant everything. Josh's dad was the town hero back in his high school days. He led the football team in its only winning season and only state championship. Ever. So of course, Josh, even though he didn't carry on the legacy his father did, still held onto the notoriety that came with it. It's like we were all judged.

CHAPTER SEVENTEEN

The party looked in full swing as we came up upon the riverbank. I could see the bonfire coming to life on the opposite bank as Josh pulled up to the river. He flipped his truck around and backed into a spot between two massive cherry red pickups. I knew nothing about trucks, whatsoever, but I thought Josh had an impressive truck. It was deep blue with chrome accents and an extended cab, or whatever you called it. But these two trucks were double the size with fog lights mounted on the top and an extra grill on the front. Even the tires were bigger.

Josh shoved the gear shift into park and looked over at me. I knew he was excited to be here and excited to be out with me in public, although I'm not sure why. We'd been hiding out all summer and I was perfectly happy to keep us hidden. This suddenly felt like a bad idea. Of course Josh would fit in here and slip right back into his old routine with his old friends, but I had no old routine or old friends. Just stale memories of people who didn't like me. I stared straight ahead back in the direction from which we came. The corn was taller than it was six weeks ago when I'd arrived. It was about chest high now and with all the headlights pointing toward the field, I could see tiny, thin ears of corn sprouting from the stalks. Josh exited the truck and slammed his door shut. In a second, he was opening my door. I didn't look at him, instead kept my focus on the corn.

"What is it?" Josh asked. He set his hand on my bare thigh

"I'm not so sure about this," I said and folded my fingers into his.

"What? Why?" Josh grabbed my face with his free hand and turned it so I was looking down at him.

"I don't know. Just because of everything. You being you, me being me, my mom, Michelle."

He just smiled and shook his head.

"Crazy girl, can't we just have fun tonight?"

I contemplated how I would be having fun. Sitting with Josh

on his truck, the same loud music blasting from all the trucks at the same time, dancing, swimming, eating, and drinking. Maybe I did need to lighten up. I wondered if Michelle would be here.

"Is Michelle going to be here?" I asked, verbalizing my thoughts.

"Uh, no. She's not." Josh looked pained as he turned away from me when he said that.

"Oh, okay then." I grabbed Josh's hand and he lifted me out of the truck. I slid down into his arms.

"You look amazing by the way," he whispered into my ear. "You've really filled out the suit nicely." I slapped him playfully for that. I did need to lighten up. I'd been telling myself all summer that I was just here for a quiet summer away, but that didn't mean I had to actually stay in the quiet of my house the whole time. I deserved to get out a little. No one would remember me anyway. Right?

Josh grabbed my hand and pulled me around to the back of his truck where a few people had already gathered. Across the river, some boys were tossing sticks into the tire rim that contained the fire.

"Josh, man! I haven't see you all summer. How's it been?" It was a boy I recognized but really couldn't remember his name.

"Hey Jake. Good. Just working a lot. You remember Jenna right?"

The boy looked at me and cocked his head to this side and studied me closely.

"Jenna. Jenna Mitchell? Wow. I haven't seen you in like two years. Where have you been?"

"Umm…"

"She's back for the summer from college," Josh said interrupting me.

"Well that's great! Welcome to the party. Grab a beer." He was really enthusiastic.

Well, that wasn't so bad. He didn't seem to know me or really remember me. Maybe this whole 'this town hates me' line of thinking was all in my head.

The sun had set by now and more trucks had arrived until the bank was completely lined with them. Those with rear face fog lights had them turned on. Every truck was tuned to the same country station and Keith Urban and Miranda Lambert blasted across the waters.

"Hey it's our song again," Josh yelled over the music

"No, this is not our song. Didn't we discuss this already?"

"But I love it!"

"It's not a love song," I mumbled back.

Josh was in a good mood tonight and I didn't want to ruin it. He was having fun dragging me around from truck to truck greeting everyone. Some people remembered me, some didn't. Some eyed me suspiciously, mostly the girls. When we made our way back to his truck, he hopped up on the tailgate and pulled me between his legs. I looked up at him and he leaned down and kissed me long and slow on the lips. His tongue flicked quickly in and out of my mouth making the butterflies in my stomach dance.

"Mmmm…You're a good kisser," I said. No one seemed to mind that I was here or that I was with Josh. Josh was happy to be out so I should be too. I mean, we had spent most of the summer shut away in my house. It was nice to be out, breathing in the warm summer air.

The bonfire was in full swing now. The flames roared so loudly that I could hear them from across the river. I looked around from my perch between Josh's legs. Most people were drinking, some were smoking. I didn't want to do either, they weren't habits I'd like to get into for several reasons. Some girls splashed around in the water hoping to coax their boyfriends to join them. I wondered how many other couples had done the deed in the river. Of course this triggered my memory of Josh and me in this very river, just a few feet from where we were now. I pictured his hard, naked body in front of me and his hands burning against my wet skin, pushing me up against the tree.

Josh let out a yelp that startled me out of my daydream. I had unknowingly dug my nails into Josh's knees.

"Hey, watch it."

"Sorry." I kissed him again.

"Were you thinking about us?" he whispered softly in my ear.

"Yes," I whispered back.

"Me too." He kissed me softly again and stared eagerly at me.

"Let's go eat something," he said and hopped off the gate. I shimmied out of my shorts and tossed them and my shirt into his truck.

"Damn," Josh said quietly just to me.

"You like?"

"Oh yeah." He put his arms around me and pulled me close to him. He unceremoniously grabbed my butt and squeezed it. "Can you feel what you're doing to me?" he whispered.

His hand moved to the small of my back, pressed my hips into his, so of course I could feel his excitement against my leg.

"Yes." I breathed into his neck. And I kissed him.

"Jenna."

"Yeah?"

"I'm hungry."

That was a strange thing to say at this moment, so I responded in agreement and pulled away from him so we could go across the river to the fire pit, but he tightened his grip effectively holding me in place.

"Not for food. For you."

His words flooded my senses. Desire flowed through my body and settled, simmering between my hips. I wrapped my arms around him and kissed over his collarbone and up his neck and finally meeting his mouth. His hand reached up and he held my chin so I couldn't move away until he was done kissing me. His kiss was deep and hard. His tongue pushed against mine sending waves of want and passion through me. I needed to get in the water quick before I burst into flames.

When Josh finally released me, he looked at me, it was dark so I couldn't see much, but the light from the bonfire created the illusion that his eyes were burning. Probably burning with the same desire that was burning in me.

"I liked that."

"Me too."

We broke apart but he still held my gaze. I walked backwards down the river bank watching him follow me eagerly. I liked this playful side to him. I hadn't seen it much at the house. He was always tense. I wondered if I made him feel that way and if being around people, around his friends, relaxed him.

We walked into the river and across to the fire pit. He had to half drag me at one point when it was neck deep. When we reached the other side, we were each handed a sharpened stick and a few hotdogs. Josh skewered mine for me and we took a spot around the pit.

"Hey," came a voice from beside me. I thought it was Josh but when I looked. It was Jake from earlier.

"Hey," I responded. I looked beyond him at Josh and he was eyeing Jake.

"So, do you have anything with you?" Jake said slowly and quietly so only I could hear him. He looked quickly to Josh and then back to me. A sly grin spread across his face.

"Um, no?" I knew instantly what he was referring to and it was exactly what I feared would happen.

"Oh. Well can you get some?"

"No. No I can't." I looked away from him. I stared into the flames hoping he'd just leave me alone.

"Are you only supplying Josh? Is that why you guys are screwing each other? Because I can guarantee I'm better than he is. And I've got a bigger…"

"Oh no. Just no." I threw my hotdog stick on the ground and stalked off to the riverbank. There was no way I was staying here any longer. I knew this was going to happen. I knew it!

"Jenna! Jenna wait!" Josh called after me, but I ignored him and made my way into the river. I tripped in the water and splashed into the river rocks at the bottom. Those suckers looked smooth and shiny, but they were actually not and I had a gash on my knee now to prove it. When Josh caught up to me, he grabbed my arm and pulled me back to him. I yanked my arm out of his grasp. I just wanted to get as far away from Jake and the other side of the river as possible. I'd like to even go home.

"Take me home, Josh! I don't want to be here anymore," I said, because I assumed Josh couldn't read my mind.

"Why? What happened?" He looked me up and down, then

looked back where we'd just came from, where Jake was standing holding all of our skewers. I couldn't make out Jake's expression in the dark, but I imagine it was a little anger, and a little worry. Everyone knew who did drugs, but no one admitted it.

I righted myself and looked at Josh. He held up his hand against the bright lights of the trucks behind me, but was staring me in the eyes. I sighed and shook my head in shame.

"Exactly what I knew would happen."

"What?"

"He wanted to buy drugs from me Josh." He brushed his hand in the air like he was brushing off the crazy notion that anyone would ever think to ask me that.

"He was probably just kidding."

"No Josh, he wasn't."

I stumbled the rest of the way out of the river and made my way to Josh's truck. I'd walk home if I had to.

"Jenna wait! Can't we just stay? Please. I haven't seen my friends all summer."

"Not my problem Josh."

I pulled on my shorts and shirt. Ugh, wet jeans and walking. Not a good combination.

"It's like three miles. Come on. Just stay."

"No."

I turned to leave and ran smack into a thick body. Why did I keep running into men? I looked up and didn't recognize him. He was tall and broad like Josh, but thicker.

"Oh, lover's spat over here? What would Michelle think?"

That was it. I was done. Why did people keep asking what Michelle would think? Maybe they should just go ask her. Maybe she could take time out of her obviously busy schedule and come see me and tell me what she thought.

"You know what?" I declared loudly. If you can't beat them, join them.

I grabbed a bottle from some girl and took a huge gulp.

"Damn, what is this?" I asked her. I didn't wait for the answer. I kept the bottle and continued to drink from it as I stumbled around the riverbank. I saw a boy light up a joint. I took it from his mouth and held it up and showed it to everyone.

"What is this? Pot? Where'd you get it? Obviously not from me!" I threw the joint at the boy I'd taken it from and stomped off toward Josh's truck. I heard Josh scramble after me, but I didn't bother to slow down. I took long swigs of the bottle of alcohol along the way.

"And who cares about Michelle?" I said randomly. "She can't even be bothered to come see me after I've been gone."

Gasps from the crowd made me turn around. Everyone was staring at me as if I'd cursed the dead or something. What the hell was going on? Whatever I was drinking was starting to affect me, I swayed a little, and Josh grabbed me.

"Get in the truck, Jenna," Josh said and ushered me toward the driver's side door. He threw it open and tossed me in harshly. He climbed in after me and gunned the engine, slammed it into gear and punched the gas, throwing dirt and rocks out behind us. I felt sorry for whoever was back there.

"What the hell was that all about?"

"Nothing. Let's just go home."

"First you refused to leave and then you throw me in your truck and hightail it out of there. I think you owe me an explanation."

"It was just time to leave."

"Josh, what the hell is going on? For real. Is this town crazy or is it me? And where the hell is Michelle?"

Josh looked over at me somberly and sighed. We were almost to my house thanks to Josh breaking the speed limit times five. He whipped into the gravel drive in front of my house and slammed on the breaks. Thank God for seatbelts.

"Dude," I said.

"Sorry."

I put my head between my legs. I was feeling sick. What the hell did I drink?

"I don't feel well."

"Shit Jenna!" I heard him get out of his truck and slam the door. My door whipped open, he reached across my lap to unlatch the seat belt and pulled me out. He half dragged me to the front door. He kicked open the front door and dumped me on the couch. It swallowed me

"Are you going to stay?" I said, or tried to.

"I don't think that's a good idea Jenna."

Without warning, tears spilled over my cheeks. I didn't even know what I was crying about, the fact that Josh was being so mean, or the whole Michelle situation. Or maybe because he wouldn't stay with me when I needed him to.

"Oh geez Jenna. What now?" I could sense the annoyance in his voice. It only made me cry harder. Josh was on the floor next to me, kneeling, with his elbows on the edge of the couch, holding his head in his hands.

"Nothing Josh. I'm fine. Thank you for depositing me at my house. You can go," I stood up from the couch and stumbled back to my bedroom. I thought about slamming the door but I secretly hoped he'd follow me back. He didn't. He must have debated with himself about it because it took him forever to make his retreat and shut my front door.

I stripped off my wet clothes and tossed them onto the tile floor of the bathroom. I'd deal with it later. I curled up under my quilt and cried myself to sleep. This night had not gone how I expected. I should have known. I should have just stayed home. I wanted a quiet summer. I should have known better about that too. I couldn't have a quiet summer here. I couldn't have anything here.

CHAPTER EIGHTEEN

Days went by and I heard nothing from Josh. No phone call, he didn't come by, no carrier pigeon. Nothing. The first day I lay in bed all day long. I was still feeling sick from whatever I drank last night. That was for sure the last time I ever drank anything, ever. Especially something from someone I didn't even know. I fell in and out of sleep and barely registered time. I didn't even know what I thought about or dreamed, everything was just a blur. I did remember that my phone was quiet. No phone calls.

The next morning I was woken up by the sound of breaking glass and a hissing noise. I rolled out of bed and stumbled to the living room. Glass covered the top of the back of the couch and a red mist hung in the air. There was also a small bottle of spray paint on the seat. I ran back to my bedroom and pulled on shorts and a t-shirt and ran out the front door. I looked around but saw no one. I tripped down the porch steps and whipped around the side of the house and stopped. The window was broken and written in spray paint across the window was the word 'HORE'. I laughed. Really? That was the best they could do? Yeah, it sucked about my window, but they hadn't even spelled whore right. Assuming that's what they were trying to spell. Under hore was 'DR'. I assumed they were about to write drug or druggie, but ran out of time or paint.

I took one last glance at the broken window before going back inside. I grabbed my phone and called Josh, but he didn't answer so I sent him a text asking him to call me. I contemplated calling Dad, but I decided to wait until after I'd talked to Josh.

I thumb tacked a doubled sheet over the window. It didn't keep the heat from seeping in, but it kept the hot air from blasting in. After I cleaned up the glass and spray paint can, I decided to keep all of it in a Ziplock bag just in case I needed it for evidence later.

I vegged out on the couch for the rest of the day contemplating what to do next. Josh never called back. I was upset and wondered if I should call the police. I didn't, instead I flipped off the TV and went to bed.

The next day I rolled out of bed when the sun hit my window. I bounded out of bed and found my phone. It was dead. Dang. I plugged it in and took a shower. I took a quick one though. I needed to know if Josh had tried to call me. He'd dumped me on the couch the day before and left me there. I didn't even know if he was mad at me or disappointed in my actions or what. Plus, I was getting more worried about the vandalism.

I snatched up my phone off the dresser. I rubbed my hands down the side of the towel I had wrapped around my body and swiped my phone open. Nothing. I slumped down on the edge of my bed. Why hadn't he called? I glanced at the time, eight AM. He'd be at work already. I dialed his number and it went straight to voicemail. His phone was off. God, was he avoiding me? That was a little drastic for him. I sent him a quick text asking him to call me or come by after work so we could talk.

I was on the edge of the couch for the rest of the day, obsessively checking my phone in the door. By evening, I was so mentally exhausted that I crawled into bed clutching my phone. The next day Andrew called several times, but I ignored them. What if Josh called or came by and I was talking to someone else? I moped around all day, I ate nothing.

I was annoyed with myself. I was being an idiot. I wasn't this girl. I didn't shut down because a guy didn't call me or come see me. I'd been through too much crap to be that girl.

Finally, after three days of no contact with Josh, I took control of myself again and showed up on his doorstep at eight o'clock at night. Mrs. Riley answered the door and silently let me in.

"Hello," I said, unsure of how to proceed. I had over-thought this entire situation and it was just ridiculous.

"Hi Jenna,"

"Is Josh here?" I asked.

"He's in his room."

"Can I see him?"

"Of course." She smiled at me then and I knew she didn't know about what had happened at the bonfire.

"Thanks." I smiled back at her then hurried down the stairs.

I heard music playing and shuffling through the closed door. I knocked softly.

"I'm not hungry mom," I heard Josh's muffled voice say.

"Um, it's me Josh."

I heard a crash and thudding before the door swung open to reveal a disheveled Josh. He was shirtless with dark blue "RHS INDIANS" sweat pants on that were tied ever so loosely around his hips. His hair was all mussed up in that way that made me forget why I was really here. Why was I here?

"What are you doing here?" he asked quickly.

"I, uh, I wanted to talk to you. About what happened at the bonfire?" I'm not sure why that last statement came out as a question.

"Oh. It's ok Jenna. These things happen."

He wouldn't look me in the eyes and he wouldn't let me in his room. He seemed distracted by something and I couldn't for the life of me think of what it could be. Work?

"What's going on Josh? You're acting strange."

"Nothing. I just don't have time to talk right now. I'm heading out."

"Heading out where?"

"It's none of your business Jenna!" He looked at me now as he yelled his last statement.

"Dude, I'm sorry." And I stalked away up the stairs. Mrs. Riley was standing at the top of the stairs, obviously listening to our conversation, if you could even call it a conversation.

"Jenna honey, wait," she said as I hurried past her. I was probably being rude, but I kind of just wanted to get out of the house. All I wanted to do was talk to Josh. I wanted to know what he was thinking about the situation and about me. And I wanted to apologize. "Jenna," Mrs. Riley said again.

"Yes," I said a little too roughly.

"Give Josh a day. He needs to sort a few things out."

"What is going on around here?"

"It's something Josh has to tell you. I can't."

"Why?"

"Because he asked me not to. I want to Jenna, but it's his situation to tell."

I leaned against the front door and looked up at the white glittery popcorn ceiling. I sighed. All this secrecy stuff was getting old. I knew it had to do with Michelle and I was mad.

"I should go before he comes upstairs," I said before opening the door and slipping out into the fading evening light.

I'd walked here so I padded down the Riley's dirt driveway and turned right onto the street that lead to home. I had to make another right turn at the end of this street before I was on the right road to home. It wasn't far, maybe fifteen minutes. Once I'd reached the end of their road, I heard Josh's truck door slam and the engine roar. He'd have to pass me to go anywhere because his street was a dead end. I secretly prayed he'd stop and pick me up. I just wanted to talk to him, to be close to him. It had been three days.

Josh's truck rumbled up the pot-holed road and stopped at the stop sign where I happened to be standing.

"Get in," I heard him yell over the diesel engine.

It was the middle of the day and the sun was blazing hot. The pavement reflected the heat back at me so there was just no relief no matter where I turned. There were thunderclouds off to the west, but I doubted they'd make it this far before it rained and we desperately needed rain. I hopped into Josh's truck. The A/C blasted and felt good on my hot skin.

Neither of us said anything to each other for the three minutes it took to drive up the hill to my house. I didn't get out right away and he didn't say anything to make me either. We just sat in silence listening to his truck rumble and idle.

"I have to go Jenna,"

"Where?" I asked quickly.

"I'll tell you later,"

"Will you?"

"Yes."

"Okay."

"What is that on your window?" he asked suddenly.

I looked over at the graffiti on the side of my house.

"It's what I was trying to talk to you about. Someone tagged my house."

Josh's face heated, his ears flaming before he threw his door open and stalked across my yard to the side of the house.

"Why didn't you tell me?" he roared.

What the hell?

"I tried Josh. I called you and texted, asking you to call me."

He paced back and forth across the lawn, glancing back up at the window.

"The window is broken?" He stopped pacing and kneeled in the grass, picking up tiny pieces of glass I hadn't thought to pick up.

"Yes."

"Who did this?"

"I don't know Josh. A bad speller?" I said mockingly. He looked at me questioningly. "Whore is spelled wrong. It's W-H-O-R-E," I spelled for him.

"Oh."

We stood there gawking at the bright red paint for a few minutes longer. I sighed. So did he.

"What Josh?"

"Nothing Jenna. This is all just really crazy and I don't have time to deal with it."

"Deal with what? I'm not asking you to do anything?"

"Then why did you want me to see it?"

"I don't know. I don't know!" I repeated. "Because you're my boyfriend and I thought you might care that someone is vandalizing my house."

"No one thinks of you like this Jenna. It's probably just a prank from the other night at the bonfire."

Was he seriously just blowing this off? I felt something drop on my head. I looked up and saw the angry grey clouds forming. It had been a beautiful clear blue sky not even ten minutes ago, and now the rain clouds hung low, ready to split open at any moment.

"Josh. Someone vandalized my house. They wrote *whore* on my house. Why are you acting like this is no big deal?"

"Well, maybe it's not."

"Oh, okay. Well if everyone in this town thinks I'm a drug-dealing whore just like my mother, maybe I should just become a drug-dealing whore."

"Jenna, you're being dramatic."

"Am I? Your life in this town was normal. Everyone loves you and you did what was expected of you. Everyone tolerated me in school because you were my friend, but I was never given the chance to show who I really am because I was overshadowed by my mother's reputation."

"Lots of people liked you."

"No, they didn't Josh. You didn't see any of it because you were too wrapped up in Michelle to ever notice what was going on with me. Not that I'm selfish enough to expect you to have."

"What's that supposed to mean?"

"It means that Michelle got boobs before me and you stopped being my friend. You only dated me to get to her. Everyone knew it. Actually, everyone thought you were screwing my mom just like your dad was."

"What the hell Jenna?"

Crap, crap,crap, I thought to myself. I never wanted to be the one to tell Josh that. Josh's look of horror told me he had no clue about his dad and my mom. I felt like the worst person in the world.

"Is that why my dad left? Did my mother know? Did he leave because of your mom?"

"Yes? I don't know Josh." Shit had hit the fan.

"Shit Jenna!" Josh punched his truck and I flinched.

"I'm sorry," I said quietly.

He laced his fingers behind his head and looked up at the sky. I did too. The sun was hidden now, but the clouds didn't do anything to stifle the heat of the afternoon. The clouds swirled swiftly around each other like they were performing their own rain dance. I contemplated making a mad dash for the front door, but Josh's phone rang, breaking into my thoughts. I looked over at him wondering about the phone call but he had ignored it again, and chose to continue to stare at the sky.

"I should just leave."

"No, this is your house, I'll go," he said and released his hands from the back of his neck.

"No, I mean I should leave town. I am causing nothing but trouble here. Everyone wants one thing from me and I can't give it to them."

"Oh Jenna, come on. Seriously? Where are you even going to go?"

"I can go back to my Dad's."

"Really? Because this whole summer you've been telling me how you're not allowed there, how your stepmom doesn't want you there blah blah blah, and now all of the sudden you can go back,?"

"Well I'm certainly not welcome here! You haven't even talked to me in days. You just stopped with no reason. I didn't even do anything!"

"I know!" Thunder cracked at the exact moment he said those words causing both of us to jump.

"Then why didn't you answer my calls?" I asked when I'd regained my composure. I felt like we were going around in circles. He wouldn't answer me, he was being secretive, and now he wouldn't even look at me.

Thunder rumbled again. We had been yelling at each other in the middle of the street in broad daylight like an old married couple. I didn't even know what to think anymore. I didn't have anywhere to go. I guess I could go to Andrew's but I'd ignored him all summer. How nice would that be; 'hey, I've been ignoring you all summer but I need a place to crash so here I am?' Um, no. I didn't roll like that.

I stood there, exasperated beyond all means and waited for Josh to respond with something legitimate. Instead, he decided to answer his phone. It had been ringing now nonstop for our entire argument. I should just hop in my car now while he was distracted and leave.

"Hello?" He sounded just as exasperated as I was. "What?" The anger in his voice evaporated. "Okay, we're on our way now."

He looked at me quickly before concentrating on the person on the other line.

"No, I don't have a choice. She's with me now. I know. Well, what do you want me to do?" he yelled the last part. He slammed the phone shut and hit the door of the truck.

Rain erupted from the sky and soaked us both instantly. I looked at the side of the house, hoping the torrential downpour would wash away the paint, but it didn't. I sighed heavily, as cool rain seeped through my clothing and chilled my skin.

"Get in the truck, Jenna," Josh said suddenly. He frowned when he looked at me. Not just a frown, he looked sad and worried. Who had he just talked to?

"Yeah right." I was not getting in a car with him now. Not after that look and not after this argument. I just wanted to get inside, dry off, crawl into bed and forget this awful day.

"Get in the damn car. We're going to see Michelle."

At the mention of Michelle's name in conjunction with Josh's mention of us going to see her, my body froze. I was stunned into non-movement. I couldn't even say no or turn back to go into my house, or even get into his truck. Why now after all this time was he taking me to see her? Where was she that I had to be driven there? She lived right down the street.

"Get in!" Josh yelled again.

I jogged around the back of the truck and hopped in the passenger's side. I'd barely gotten my seatbelt fastened before Josh floored the gas pedal and sped down the road, taking corners without slowing down.

"Where are we going?" I asked.

"You'll see." That was all I got. He stared straight ahead, his mouth fixed in a thin line, his forehead wrinkled with worry. He slowed finally and turned into the hospital. The hospital.

"Josh why are we at the hospital?" What the hell was going on? A million questions flew through my head. Was Michelle in an accident? Was it her dad, her mom? We didn't turn into the emergency entrance like I thought we would. So Michelle was here, but not because of an emergency. He pulled around to the back of the hospital and parked. He didn't make a move to get out. Instead he sat there with his hands on the steering wheel staring at the brick wall in front of us, into nothingness.

"Josh?" It wasn't really a question. Of course, I was curious, but I'd just been tossed around in his speeding truck.

"Just come on," he said. He stalked toward the door without waiting for me so I scrambled out and ran up the walkway behind him.

We wound through the bright white hallways and took a cramped elevator to the fourth floor. A few more turns dropped us at a huge rounded front desk where five or so nurses sat clicking away at computers or filling out medical charts. A couple of them smiled at Josh as we passed and threw me strange looks. He ignored them all and paused in front of room 427. The door was half-open and several voices floated out.

Josh pushed the door open. I grabbed his hand when I heard Mayor Banks' voice. I knew he was behind the crazy man who broke into my house, but I had no proof.

"I don't think I should be here," I said.

"Yes, you should."

And we went in.

CHAPTER NINETEEN

The hospital room was huge. Probably half the size of my house. No, not really, but close. A hospital bed was over in one corner where Josh's mom, Michelle's mom, and Michelle's sister Renee stood on one side. The curtains were pulled back revealing a rain-streaked window. I bet they had it open to let the sun in earlier. Josh took my hand and led me to the bed where I knew Michelle laid. Even though it was a hospital room, it looked more like her room at home but with about fifty flower arrangements. Pictures of Michelle and her friends lined what little shelf space there was along with small bears and other stuffed animals. I tried to look closely at the pictures, but Josh's hand on my lower back guided me to the bed, forcing me to look at Michelle.

Her long hair was the same red I always remembered. It had been brushed and tucked underneath her. Her fair, flawless skin was paler than I remembered and her cheeks were sunken in. What had happened? Cords and wires snaked out from under the hospital gown and blankets. Machines beeped and whirred, tracking Michelle's every breath, every movement, even if we could see it with our own eyes.

I looked up at Josh's mom, she had her arm wrapped around Michelle's mom. Renee had her arm around her other side. Tears streamed down all their faces. Despite the tears, Renee seemed to be smiling. Was this a happy moment? It sure wasn't for me. I was scared out of my mind. What the hell was going on? Why was Michelle here? What had happened to her? Was she dying? Why had no one told me? The same questions circled around in my head.

"What happened?" I whispered to Josh. I was too stunned to be mad right at this moment.

Despite my attempt to stay quiet, my voice disrupted the family moment and Michelle's mother looked up at me. I shrunk back behind Josh. I was unsure what Mrs. Banks thought of me after the scandal with my mother happened. I knew she was the one who found her husband strung out on drugs in bed with my mother, and she was devastated.

"Jenna," Mrs. Banks said through sobs. "Oh Jenna. Come here sweetheart." She broke away from Mrs. Riley and Renee and stretched her arms out to me. I met her and let her hug me.

"Jenna. You and Michelle were best friends. I tried to get a hold of you, but none of the numbers Michelle had were good." Her words rushed out and I barely caught what she was saying.

"I-I'm sorry? I left my phone here when I left Riverview. Mrs. Banks, what happened?" I asked.

"Josh hasn't told you?"

I looked at Josh then back to Mrs. Banks. "No." I looked over at Mrs. Riley too.

"Michelle was in a car accident shortly after you left. The night you left in fact. She was upset about her father and me and just drove away. We still aren't sure what happened but she swerved off the road and into the Crystal Springs Bridge. She nearly went into the river. She's been here ever since."

The Crystal Springs Bridge spanned the river at the edge of town; you had to cross it from the highway to get into town.

I imagined what my face looked like to her. Shock, shame, fear, sadness, anger. Tears threatened and a lump formed at the back of my throat. My best friend had been in a coma for a year and a half while I pranced around in college. While I was bitter about her never contacting me. While I was angry with her when I came back here and she didn't come see me and how Josh kept me from her. While I cozied up to Josh. While I had sex with him.

Josh.

He had kept me from her.

Jack. Ass.

Now I was angry with Josh. I hugged Mrs. Banks again, this time a little tighter.

"I'm so sorry; I had no idea."

"I heard you were back in town and wondered why you hadn't come to see her, or even stopped by the house."

"I didn't know," I said again, shooting a glare at Josh. "So what happened tonight? Why the mad rush? Is she okay?" I'd moved away from Josh. I was so mad at him.

"She woke up," Renee said.

"Oh wow. Well that's good, right?"

"Yeah. But we've had a few false hopes."

"I see." I stared down at Michelle. She'd lost weight. She had always been a little on the chubby side. When I stayed the night at her house, we would compare notes. She wanted to be skinny like I was and I wanted nice boobs like hers. I laughed a little at the memory.

"So she's waking up?" I asked.

"Well, her monitors spiked early this morning. They have been all summer actually. The first time it happened we didn't leave her room for three days, in hopes that she'd wake up,"

"Like brain activity spikes?"

"Yes and bodily movements. Involuntary movements are normal, but some of her nurses have seen her raise her hands up and reach for something," Renee said.

"I see." I knew from my limited knowledge of psychology that these activities could really mean anything. She could be waking up, or her brain could just be stimulated by food or medications or anything really.

"May I talk to her?" I asked. I had so many things I wanted to say to her. I wanted to tell her about my time in college, about Andrew, about how much I'd missed her. I wanted to tell her about Josh, but I wasn't sure if that was a good idea. Mostly I just wanted to hear her voice, but that seemed a little impossible now.

"Of course you can honey," Mrs. Banks said. She ushered me toward the bed. I heard Josh cough and shuffle behind me but I ignored him.

I walked over to her bed and sat down in the folding chair that was set up next to it. The sheets were wrinkled under her hands so I straightened them. I brushed her hand and it twitched, so I grabbed it.

"Michelle? Michelle, it's Jenna. I'm here." I was suddenly at a loss for words. After all the conversations I'd had in my head with her, after all the times I knew what I wanted to say to her, I had nothing. "I moved back for the summer. I'm sorry I didn't come visit you sooner, I didn't know you were here. I didn't know anything. I'm so sorry." Tears burst from my eyes and I pressed her hand to my damp cheek. "I'm so sorry."

I sat like this for only a few minutes before her hand twitched again. I looked over at Mrs. Banks and Mrs. Riley. I had no clue where Josh was. Probably still behind me.

"Michelle?" I said again. A few more minutes passed before I heard a faint whisper or maybe a cough.

"Michelle?" My voice was all high and breaking with tears.

She turned her head slowly to me; it was like something out of a horror movie. If she wasn't my best friend, I'd think she would spew green goo all over me at any minute. Her eyes fluttered open and locked with mine.

"I was expecting Channing Tatum," she croaked.

Stunned by her choice of words, I was speechless. I looked to the moms, then to Renee, hoping they'd have some kind of explanation.

"I'm sorry?" What else was I supposed to say?

Everyone shifted uncomfortably. Renee let out a small cough from across the room that sounded suspiciously like she was covering up a laugh. Is this really what people say when they wake up from a coma?

"Sweetheart. Do you know where you are?" Mrs. Banks asked, moving beside me. I wanted to get up and let her sit beside her daughter, but she had her hand on my shoulder, effectively holding me in place.

"Yes. I'm in a hospital," she said matter of factually.

Everyone shifted again. Michelle looked from me up to the ceiling. She was extremely coherent for just waking up.

"How long have you been awake?" I asked.

"She just opened her eyes," Josh said from behind me.

"Thank you Captain Obvious," I said, not looking at him.

"Since you came back to town," she said quickly before I could say anything else.

"How do you know when I came back?"

"Josh told me."

I turned around I shot a glance at Josh.

"What do you mean, sweetheart?" Mrs. Banks asked.

"I've been able to hear what's been going on for a while now. I mean, I guess a while, I haven't exactly been able to tell time." Her voice was hoarse and scratchy. I wanted to tell her to stop talking, but I was too baffled to say anything.

"Oh honey, why didn't you just tell us?" Mrs. Banks asked again.

"I wanted to, but I couldn't." She was still staring at the ceiling.

What else had he told her while he thought she was asleep? Is that why she wasn't looking at me? I was ashamed of my actions this summer. I'd completely blown off my best friend and then slept with her boyfriend. I hadn't even inquired about her any further than Josh. I was a terrible friend.

"That's weird," I said, unable to form normal thoughts.

"If you'd kissed me I might have woken up sooner," Michelle quipped.

This time Renee did laugh and so did her mom.

"What else did Josh tell you?"

"Nothing really. He hasn't been around much lately."

"I see." I looked back at Josh again.

Several nurses and doctors came in at that moment. Mrs. Riley had gone to notify them that Michelle had woken up. I moved back away from her bed and rejoined Josh at the back of the room. He grabbed my hand and pulled me into the hallway.

"She doesn't know anything else about us," he said quietly, like Michelle could still hear us. She couldn't.

"Why did you keep this from me?" I was livid. I could barely contain the anger I felt at this moment.

Josh just stared at me like I'd grown a third arm or something. But really, why had he kept this from me? He'd listened to me for weeks now talk about how I missed Michelle and how I was angry she hadn't called. He'd specifically told me not to call her or go see her. Even after her dad attacked me, he still urged me not to contact her.

"I don't know," he finally said after the longest pause ever.

"This is insane Josh. Michelle was, is my best friend. I had a right to know she'd been lying in a coma for a year and half. God, Josh. Why did you think it was okay to do this? It wasn't your place." I was yelling now, tears threatened behind my eyes.

"Keep your voice down."

"Oh no. You don't get to tell me what to do anymore."

"Jenna," Josh reached for me but I pulled away.

"No."

I turned away from him and went back into Michelle's room. The doctors and nurses were still huddled around her bed, but I could see that she was sitting up now. A wave of memories flooded my mind and the threatening tears spilled down my cheeks.

Michelle and I had over a decade of memories together. We'd met one day when my mom sent me out of the house for some reason, probably a guy or drugs, or both. I didn't know where to go so I just walked. After wandering the town for over an hour, I found a playground and parked myself on the swings. I hooked my arms around the chains and leaned forward so I swung slowly back and forth and dragged my feet in the dirt. I was watching the grass grow when a pair of hot pink glittery flip flops came into view. When I glanced up to meet the owner of the shoes, I was met with a smile.

"I'm Michelle, want to be friends?"

And that was that. We played for hours at the park that day. Michelle was full of imagination and she taught me how to use mine. The teeter totter was really a space launcher, the slide took us to an underground jewel mine where we dug up diamonds and rubies and became princesses. Eventually her dad came to pick her up. Michelle asked if he would take me home too but he said no. It wasn't the last I saw of Michelle though. That summer we spent every waking moment together. Even some non-waking moments. Her mom was kind and loved having me over, her dad on the other hand, did not. Neither of us cared though.

I stood awkwardly in the hospital room, reliving our memories and watched the doctors poke and prod at her. Mrs. Riley and Mrs. Banks stood at the end of the bed, watching everything too.

"Do you want to go to the cafeteria?" Renee asked, startling me.

"Um, no. I think I'll just go home. Can I come back tomorrow though?"

"Of course you can. Your presence seems to have awakened her. And she wants you here," Mrs. Banks said as she came up beside us.

"Okay. Thanks." We hugged and I turned to leave. Josh followed me to the door too.

"Don't follow me," I said and blocked him with my hand.

"I drove you here," he said.

Crap.

"Okay. Take me home. Now." There was no need for politeness anymore.

We walked silently through the hallways, down the elevator, and out to his truck. The ride was equally as quiet. In fact, I didn't even say anything before I slammed the truck door and ran to my front door. I was too hurt and too embarrassed.

CHAPTER TWENTY

I'd been parked on the couch for over an hour staring mindlessly at some reality show on the TV. It had been raining for two days now. I really wanted to go to the river, I needed to clear my thoughts. But after two days of raining, the banks would be overflowing with water, and the current would be stronger. I read *Bridge to Terabithia*, I knew what happened to girls who fell in rivers.

Instead, I moped around the house, dwelling on the images of Michelle laying there motionless in the hospital room. I just couldn't imagine her being like that for a year and a half. I felt like a terrible friend. I hadn't called or even tried to contact her the entire time I was gone, and when I came back I assumed she'd call me. Then when Josh told me not to call her, I assumed she didn't want to talk to me, that she hated me. I shouldn't assume things and I shouldn't listen to boys. Ugh, Josh! Why didn't he tell me? Who was he protecting? Me or her? Or both? I didn't want to think about that. I was still mad at him.

I didn't go see Michelle until three days later. I just couldn't get myself up off the couch. I used the rain as an excuse, but really I was doing some self-hating, and wallowing in my own self-pity. I was turning into someone I didn't like. Josh was affecting more than I liked, in the wrong ways. I liked it when he was close to me and touched me in a way that stirred desire inside me. I liked his lips on mine and the way he held my face when we kissed. All good things end. I must take the bad with the good I guess. I just wish there didn't have to be a bad with Josh. My feelings for him had grown. I'd seriously contemplated staying here to be with him, or at least give Andrew a heads up that we weren't going to be anything more than friends.

God this sucked.

The sun had set by the time I even thought about moving. There must have been a marathon of this show, because the same characters were on. I wandered into the kitchen and opened the fridge and stared. I had nothing but left-over frozen meals. I didn't want to eat them, I didn't want to think of Josh, and frozen food reminded me of him.

The doorbell rang, startling me. I was 99% sure it was Josh and 99% sure I didn't want to talk to him. Instead of listening to my 99%, I went to the door and answered it. Well, I was right, it was Josh, and I let him in. The stupid 1%.

"Hey Jen," he said softly.

"Hey."

"Can we talk?"

So when I'd needed him last week he'd ignored my calls and texts and blew me off when I showed up at his house, but now he needed to talk to me and suddenly everything's supposed to be all okay? No thank you. I was all ready to blow him off, but then he looked at me with those painfully blue eyes full of sadness and I just couldn't say no.

"You can talk. I'm not really interested in talking to you," I said finally and moved aside so he could come in the house.

"Come on Jenna."

"'Come on Jenna'? Come on Josh! What the hell Josh? What the hell? My best friend is in a freaking coma and you didn't think it was a good idea to tell me? What the freaking hell!"

"I'm sorry."

"No, you're an idiot. What did you think? That you could get away with it because I wasn't staying past August? That you could just have your cake and eat it too?"

"Jenna."

"What?" I no longer liked the way he said my name.

I paced around the living room making grand gestures and flailing my arms around. I was pissed and rightfully so. I came around again and stood in front of him. He was much taller than me so my attempt at a forceful, angry stance felt a little silly, but I held my ground and glared at him with narrowed eyes.

"Jenna, you said you weren't here to start trouble, that you wanted a quiet summer. I was trying to give you that."

"I wanted my friends. I wanted to talk to Michelle! You knew that!"

"Well, she was in a coma and you couldn't have her anyway!"

"Did you know that she's been awake for like, weeks now? She's heard everything you've said."

"Yeah, but I didn't tell her about us."

"That's not the point!"

"Then what is?" He was exasperated now.

"The point is that you had no right to keep me from her."

"I was going to tell you. I was. When the doctors said she might be waking up, I was going to tell you, but then that guy ransacked your house and I thought it would be better just to leave it for now. And now you think her dad is behind the whole thing. What if you two ran into each other at the hospital? What would you do? What do you think he'd do? You haven't heard the rumors Jenna. People are saying that you slept with the mayor." He sounded like he believed the rumor and was waiting for me to confirm it.

"What?" I was horrified at this admission, but not surprised at the same time.

Not only was it not true, but I knew exactly who started it. Mayor Banks. Even though I didn't turn him in as the 'robber' who broke into my house, he'd sent out a preemptive strike against me. This all but proved he was behind the whole thing. "What other rumors are out there?" I asked.

"Just that, and that you are selling drugs for sex just like your mom."

"Damn it! Damn it!" I slumped down on the couch and hung my head between my legs. I was done. I knew I shouldn't have come back here. I should not have gone to see my mom. Then the mayor would have gotten his drugs when he came by and all would be good. Or he would have turned me in for drug possession and my life would have been over.

A disgusting thought popped into my head. A thought I didn't want to think. A thought so unthinkable it made me want to vomit.

"Josh," I said after a bit.

"Yes?" My head was still lowered but I felt him rush to me. The couch cushions dipped when he sat next to me.

"Is she why you hung out with me all summer? Did you want

to be with me so you'd know where I was all the time, so I wouldn't find out about her?

He shifted beside me and took a really long time to answer. I didn't need his answer, I knew.

"No Jenna."

"Liar!" I said and got up from the couch, leaving him staring after me.

"I'm not, Jenna. Jenna, please?" He got up off the couch and stood in front of me so I had to look at him. He was hunched over so he was eye level with me and his arms were at his sides, his hands palm side up. He was asking my forgiveness.

"I liked you Josh. I said I loved you." Tears threatened, but I would not allow myself to cry about this. I'd held on to Josh as some kind of enigma. He was my childhood sweetheart and I thought he would save me from this town, from my life. But I was wrong. So wrong.

"Jenna, I'm sorry. I never wanted it to play out like this. Jenna, I love you, I always have. Michelle and I are over, I promise. I love you, Jenna." His words meant nothing to me anymore.

He followed me as I paced around the house. I stalked into the kitchen, then through the bedroom and back into the living room. He was right behind me. I could feel his breath on the back of my neck.

"Jenna," he said again.

"Please get out of my house," I said firmly. I stood with my arms crossed and my back straight. I was for real this time.

"Jenna, please?" The way he said my name sent a familiar sensation down my spine but I ignored it.

I was angry, and hurt, and sad, and frustrated, and lonely, and broken. I thought I was in love with Josh. I had given myself to him. I had shared everything with him. He was the only thing in this town that didn't suck for me and now it was ruined.

"Please just go," I said. I walked around him, back to my room.

I heard the heavy oak door creak open then the slam of the storm door as he left.

I snatched up my phone, dove under the blankets and dialed the number I'd been avoiding all summer. It rang twice the clicked on.

"Hello?" The deep, familiar voice said.

"Andrew?" I couldn't suppress my tear any longer. They burst from my lips and I cried into the phone until I had no tears left.

CHAPTER TWENTY-ONE

I woke up the next morning to a damp pillow. My fingers were still curled around my phone and my eyes were dry and scratchy. My foggy mind tried to piece together what had happened. Fight with Josh, lots of tears, called Andrew. Oh God. I called Andrew. I looked at my phone and a call was still in session...

"Andrew?" I said quietly

"Right here babe." I liked it when he called me that. Josh had called me babe once and it was just weird and awkward. Thoughts of Josh reminded me that he was the reason for the tears last night.

"Have you been on the phone this whole time?" I said as I held back the tears.

"Yep. And you snore."

"Shut up. I do not," I laughed.

"You do and it's adorable."

I sat up on my bed and wiped the tears that had slipped out. I sighed heavily and took my phone with me to the bathroom. I caught a glimpse of myself in the mirror. A tangled halo of hair circled my head, my eyes were bloodshot, and my nose was bright red. I don't usually get the 'cry face' but after last night, I'm not surprised.

"Andrew." I said to myself in the mirror.

"Yeah babe," he said back from the phone.

"I miss you."

"I miss you too. When are you coming back?"

"Real soon."

"Good."

"Okay, I'm going to go get dressed. I have a few things to take care of here before I can leave."

"Sure thing, babe. I'm glad you called."

"Sorry I've been ignoring you."

"It's okay."

"No, it's not. I'm sorry."

"Are you going to be ok? Do you want to talk about it?

"Not right now. I have to sort it all out in my head.

"Okay. Hurry back."

"Yeah."

With that, I hung up with Andrew. I was an idiot. I had a good thing going with Andrew. Even if we weren't 'a thing', we were something. Andrew had been nothing but nice to me. He believed what I'd told him and didn't press the matter when I said I didn't want to talk about it. I was being a child about this whole situation. It wasn't even that bad. So I'd had a crappy childhood. Many kids did. I wasn't special. I didn't deserve special treatment because of the life I'd been given. But I also didn't deserve the treatment I'd been given from this town. I was not my mother, and I had never shown this town any indication that I would turn into her.

I slammed the phone down on my bed and stood up quickly. I needed to stop acting like an idiot and take my life back into my own hands. I could rise above this shitty town and show them that I was better. I would not run away again like last time. I was not here to stay, but for the rest of my time here, I would show them who I really was. I wasn't a whore, or a drug dealer, or a girl who sits around feeling sorry for herself. No. I was an overcomer. I had people in my life who loved me and cared about me and needed me. From now on I would focus on that.

I needed to go see Michelle. I knew Josh said that the two of them were over, but if Michelle's mom called Josh and his mom to come to the hospital when Michelle woke up, then something must still be there between them. I pulled on jeans and a t-shirt, ran a comb through my hair, and skipped the bathroom mirror. I just hoped my face returned to normal before I had to see people.

The trip to the hospital was too short. I wondered if Josh or Mayor Banks would be there. With my newfound determination, I rather hoped they would both be there. I wanted to tell them what I really thought of them now. But the hospital probably wasn't the time or place to bring up the fact that I'd slept with Josh, and that I was accusing Michelle's dad of orchestrating an attack on me in my home because of some old drugs that were still in my house.

I sat in my car a while before finally getting out. I slammed the door shut to let out a little frustration before stalking into the hospital. When I reached her room, I heard low voices, there were a lot of people in there. I guess her mom and sister, and a voice I didn't recognize, then I heard the mayor's voice. Shit, all my determination and self-resolve left me. I didn't want to confront the mayor. Not now. I almost turned to leave, but my need to see Michelle again got the better of me. Besides, Renee and Mrs. Banks wouldn't let anything happen. I pushed the door open slowly and peaked inside. Crap. There was the mayor. I opened the door more and saw that Renee and Mrs. Banks stood on one side of the bed, while Mayor Banks was talking animatedly. I looked around some more, Josh was standing by the window. Double shit. The door creaked and everyone turned to look at me. Triple shit. I was about to make my exit.

Mayor Banks hurried toward the door. He looked like he was going to run me down, so I backed away a little.

"Jenna, you are not welcome here. You are the reason she's in this place to begin with," he yelled.

"Dad! Stop! Jenna can come in."

"No. This is a family matter and she is not family."

"Dad."

"Honey, it's okay," Mrs. Banks said.

Mayor Banks glared at me then backed back into Michelle's room. I followed him and took a place next to Michelle's bed. I leaned down to hug her and I heard her dad scoff behind me.

"How's it going?" I asked.

"Good. I need to stay here for a couple more weeks, then I get to go home," she said. Her voice was sounding stronger.

"That's good."

"Yeah. My vitals have stayed steady for the past few weeks while I was asleep, and for the last few days nothing has really changed, so the doctors think it's okay for me to go home if I keep a low profile and don't try to do too much too soon. I've lost muscle tone so I'm not as strong as I was, so I'll need to do physical therapy, but I can do that at home as well."

"Yeah, no swinging off the rope swing into the river," Josh

laughed. It quickly fizzled into a cough, his face distorted into a million different emotions all at once when he looked away from me. The river. That's what he was thinking about. He couldn't even look at me anymore. Ouch. The once beautiful and most meaningful memory of the two of us was now marred and dirty. He kept his gaze from me. I'm not sure if Michelle caught our exchange, if she did, she didn't say anything.

"Well you won't be going anywhere with her. You'll be staying at home. Jenna's leaving soon anyway, aren't you Jenna?" the mayor said.

The way he said my name, full of disdain. I hated it.

"Yes," I smiled. "I'm heading back to school."

"Where she can't hurt you anymore," he said to Michelle.

"Dad, stop. How many times do I have to tell you that it wasn't Jenna's fault? It was yours. You slept with her mom. You got caught with the drugs. You should be in jail right along with Jenna's mom. But you're not." Everyone in the room grew quiet at Michelle's outburst. "And I know you sent that man over to her house to steal back the drugs that were still in her house."

I looked from Michelle to her dad. His face was contorted into a look of horror. His mouth gaped open and closed like a fish. He was trying to say something to defend himself but apparently could not come up with a good enough lie to cover up the truth his daughter just spilt.

"Um," I said randomly.

"Oh yeah, I've heard everything. All things. Mom, you should really just leave him." She sat back in her bed and folded her arms. She glared at her father for a moment longer, then dismissed him. She stared out the window.

The horrified looks on everyone's faces were enough to tell me that they'd all heard the rumors too. I wondered what Mrs. Riley was thinking. She'd been the one I'd run to after Mayor Banks had attacked me. I bet she knew the rumor wasn't true.

"Michelle honey, you should rest. You don't want to overexert yourself," Mrs. Banks said. She flitted around Michelle's bed, fixing the sheets and Michelle's hair.

"I'm fine Mom." She threw her hands up, effectively stopping her mother's fretting. "I'm just saying what everyone is thinking."

It was true. Michelle had just exposed her father as a liar, a thief, and basically a drug dealer. This was the proof I needed that my suspicions about the mayor being behind the attack were true. But would anyone believe a girl who'd be in a coma for over a year? I doubted it, but I had a room full of witnesses who'd seen his reaction to Michelle's accusatory words.

"You are lying. There's no way you could have possibly heard that," Mayor Banks said hurriedly.

"Maybe not, but you just kind of admitted to saying them."

The mayor took a few steps back from where he was standing next to his wife. Mrs. Banks was glaring at him along with Michelle, Josh and myself.

"No one is going to believe you. Any of you." And he turned and walked quickly out of the room.

There were several seconds of silence. Michelle had relaxed again against the headboard of her bed, Mrs. Banks had her eyes closed and was mouthing something to herself.

"Should we call the police?" I asked breaking the silence.

"No. That won't do any good. He's got the police in this town in his coat pocket. I've had divorce papers drawn up for over a year now. I just didn't want to serve them to him while you were in the hospital," Mrs. Banks said.

"How will that solve anything?" I asked looking from Mrs. Banks to Michelle.

"I'm the one who has all the money. I inherited it from my father who was the Mayor of Riverview in its heyday," she said almost offhandedly.

"What about his money?" I asked

"He squanders it. I pay the bills. The house is mine. My kids are grown now. Michelle will need care after she is released, but I can handle that. He will not be a problem anymore. We are done."

The tension in the room hung thick in the air. No one knew what to say or do. I felt awkward in the room. Huge secrets had just been spilled. I heard the door click softly and I turned to see a doctor walk in and began to assess Michelle. He looked over her chart and turned to Mrs. Banks.

"Her vitals are looking good. I'd like to continue with the clear liquids for now. She's been on the feeding tube for over a year now, so introducing foods slowly through the mouth is what we'd like to do." He looked around the room awkwardly. This doctor had no idea what he'd just walked into. "Okay then. I'll have a nurse bring you the menu so that you know what your choices are."

"When will she be able to go home?" Mayor Banks asked. We all looked to him as he stormed back through the door he had just left through.

"Well, she's only been awake for a week now."

"She can recover at home. I don't want her here where anyone can just drop in whenever they want." There was no doubt who he was talking about. Me.

"That's not ideal. We need her to be able to eat normally and she'll be starting physical therapy this week. Her first few days will be intense and painful, it would be best if she were here during that time," the doctor countered.

"She can do everything at home," the mayor said again.

"No. She will stay here until the recommended time. I will not go against doctor's orders. And it's not up to you who can visit her. As far as I'm concerned, you are no longer part of this family!"

"Mom! Dad!" Michelle screamed.

We all looked at her just in time to see her vomit over the side of the bed.

"I need everyone to leave the room please."

Mayor Banks pushed his way over to Michelle, but the doctor beat him to her.

"I mean everyone."

The mayor held back his words and stormed out of the room for a second time, brushing past me, almost knocking me over. When I left the room with Mrs. Banks, he was nowhere to be seen.

"What happened?" I asked.

"I think she got a little over stimulated. And the whole food thing is stressing her out. She doesn't want to be in here because she doesn't want to see her dad."

"I can understand that," was all I could think to say in response. "I think I'm going to just go home now."

"Okay Honey. I'll call you if anything changes. We'll stay."

"I'll stay too," Josh said.

I just looked at him silently. I didn't have anything else to say to him.

"Bye," I said to Mrs. Banks, but ignored Josh.

"I'll walk you out," he said. I didn't even want to argue, so I let him follow me.

When we got to the front door of the hospital, he stopped me. "Jenna, can I come by tomorrow?" he asked, his eyes pleading with me.

"Sure," I replied.

I didn't have anything more to say to him. He'd lied to me in a huge way and he'd broken my heart. There wasn't much else he could do now, except break it more.

CHAPTER TWENTY-TWO

A week had gone by and Michelle had recovered enough to be released to go home with a twenty-four hour nurse. I'd seen her on the day she left the hospital and helped her pack up her room, but I hadn't been to the house since she'd been home. Mayor Banks had refused to leave the house or sign the divorce papers so, Mrs. Banks was in the process of getting a restraining order against him.

I'd contemplated leaving town for days, but I couldn't leave without seeing Michelle again. I didn't want to leave again without saying goodbye, not like last time

Josh hadn't come by like he'd said he would, which didn't surprise me. I was hurt and I didn't know who to turn to. I didn't want to spill everything to Andrew just yet. My only other two friends I could talk to about my problems were Josh and Michelle, I couldn't really talk to Josh about this because it was about him, and Michelle had her own set of problems to deal with and didn't need mine thrown in the mix.

I was currently packing and sorting through things, when I heard a knock on my bedroom door. I almost jumped out of my skin.

"What the hell, Josh!" I screamed.

"Sorry. You didn't hear me knock on the front door, so I let myself in. You shouldn't leave your doors unlocked."

"What do you want?" I asked.

"I'm sorry I haven't been by," he said. He really did look sorry. I should probably give him a second chance.

That whole day when I first saw Michelle was so overwhelming. I hadn't even given him a chance to explain himself. I had done some rational thinking and realized that Josh was only trying to protect Michelle and me. He thought he was doing what was best, and after the mayor had told me to stay away as well, he must have felt like he was doing the right thing. I'd decided not to be mad at him anymore just for the sake of leaving on good terms. Besides, I really did love him and we'd shared an intimate, meaningful summer. I owed him that.

"Jenna, I'm going to stay with Michelle. She needs me right now," Josh blurted out interrupting my thoughts.

I locked eyes with him as I stood, rooted to the spot in the middle of my room. I was lost for words. I was about to burst with sadness. I'd opened myself up to him this summer like I never had to anyone before. He had reached in and held my heart. Now, he was slowly crushing it with every word he spoke. I had just reconciled with him in my head and now he was ruining everything.

"What?" I finally said.

"I'm sorry, Jenna."

I had always known we wouldn't make it past the summer, but there was still that small part of me that held on to hope. Hope that we could work it out and wait for each other, but his lies had prevented that, and now this. After everything we'd shared these past few months, heck, our whole lives, now he was backing out on me again? And this time it was his own decision. His mom wasn't forcing him to break up with me, no peer pressure from his friends. Josh had come to the conclusion on his own that for some reason Michelle needed him and he was going to leave me for her.

"Jenna, I'm sorry. I feel responsible for what happened to her," he said.

"How? Were you driving the car?"

"Well, no. But--"

"No. Just no," I interrupted.

I pushed past him on my way out the door. I couldn't stand to be in the same room as him any longer. I didn't even want to argue with him anymore. I ran as fast as I could, not caring where I was going. I passed house after house until there were no more houses to pass. I stopped and looked around. I was at the playground. The same playground where I'd first met Michelle. I walked up to the swing I'd been sitting on that day. The chains were rusty, but the seat was intact. I tested it out with my knee before I turned around to sit. It held my weight, so I started swinging. Not fast, just enough to feel the wind on my face then I leaned forward and dragged my feet on the ground.

White sandaled feet entered my field of vision. Her toes were hot pink and glittery.

"Michelle, what are you doing out here?" I asked, surprised

"My mom is smothering me, I needed to get out of the house."

I laughed. So did she. She sat in the swing next to me and swung a little before stopping to talk again.

"So what are you doing out here?" Michelle asked.

I looked up at her. She wore white shorts and a pale pink collared shirt. Her red hair was pulled back low on her neck and she squinted in the early afternoon sun.

"Josh and I had an argument."

"Oh really?" She seemed genuinely surprised. "What about?"

"You."

"Me? What about me?"

I wondered in that moment how much Michelle knew about Josh and me and what we'd been doing all summer.

"What has Josh told you about us?"

"About you two? He told me that you kept him company and that you made him watch Disney Princess movies. Which is awesome by the way because he never let me watch what I wanted."

"And that's all he told you?"

Her face scrunched up so she looked like a squirrel. Yep, that was it, Josh had totally not told her anything. God that sucked. It hurt too. My already crumbling heart was losing even more pieces. How was Michelle going to take it when I told her Josh and I had had sex? How would my heart take it? I'd just gotten her back and now I'd probably lose her again.

"Michelle," I said and looked right at her. "Josh and I did more than just watch movies all summer. He was at my house like every day. He took me out. We had sex." I wanted to look away from her, but I kept my eyes on her. She looked out across the playground. She was trying to keep her face steady, but her eye twitched and filled with tears and her chin quivered.

She stood up from the swings and started off across the park toward her house.

"Michelle! Michelle, wait!"

"No! How could you do this to me? I loved him, I was in love with him!"

"Michelle, I had no idea. I didn't even know you were still in town! Besides he told me you weren't even together anymore"

"Yeah well you should have made sure!"

"I was going to but your dad cornered me at Miller's and threatened me, and then Josh told me not to contact you, and when you didn't either I just assumed you weren't around anymore or just didn't want to talk to me."

"I couldn't contact you, I was lying in a hospital bed unconscious!"

"But I didn't know that!"

"This is so messed up!" Michelle crashed to the ground on her knees, sobbing. I knelt beside her, not sure if I should touch her or leave her.

"I am so sorry. You have to know that I would never hurt you. Never. That's not who I am."

Michelle didn't respond, she just stayed on the ground, her body shuddered and shook with her tears. I couldn't keep mine in anymore and I let them spill down my cheeks in silence.

"Jenna."

"Yeah?"

"I'm sorry."

"What?"

She looked over at me, her eyes were red and puffy, and she could use a tissue.

"I'm sorry I wasn't a better friend to you when you were here."

"Michelle, you were the best friend I ever had. How can you say that?"

"I don't know."

"Well, I'm sorry for sleeping with Josh."

"Do you love him?" she asked.

"I thought I did. But now I'm not so sure. He's not who I thought he was."

"Jenna, Josh and I had broken up before you were sent away to live with your dad. We weren't working out. Not because he wasn't a good guy, but because he wanted to stay here and I wanted to leave. I wanted you and me to go off to college together and have adventures and leave this small town behind us."

"Oh wow."

"Yeah. And that day you left, the day of my accident, I was coming to find you to tell you my plan. It had nothing to do with my parents. Well, maybe a little. I wanted to get away from them. I wanted to be with you. I didn't want you to forget me."

"Oh Michelle, I never would have forgotten you!"

We were both crying at that point.

"So what happened?" I asked.

"I honestly really don't know, Jenna. My parents, the doctors, and the police have all asked me, but I just don't remember."

"An animal maybe? Did you swerve to miss one?"

"Maybe? Believe me, I've thought about it for hours and hours but there's nothing there. I remember wanting to go see you, and then I remember hearing Josh's voice telling me you were back in town."

"Oh wow. That's crazy. That must have been scary."

"Yeah. I couldn't move or speak, only listen. I mean, I had some sense of what was going on, like I just knew what was happening, but not why it was happening."

"That's weird."

We were silent for a while and just sat on the ground next to each other, our legs stretched out in front of us on the rough grass. The sun hit our legs, she was white and pale from lack of exposure, while I on the other hand, had a nice tan going.

"Josh really isn't a bad guy you know," she said.

"Oh Michelle. I know. I know. He's just misguided and confused. I think he's at my house right now."

"Really?"

"Yeah. He pissed me off so I ran."

"You ran here? Away from Josh?"

"Yeah." It sounded silly when she said it out loud. I laughed.

"What are you going to do about him?" she asked.

"We're done. I'm done. Done with this town. There's nothing left for me here, Michelle."

"I'm here." She looked over at me, her eyes narrowed because of the sun.

"I know."

"I want to come with you."

"What do you mean?"

"To Brookhaven, to college. My plan. We should do my plan!"

"Oh Michelle, what about your mom and your head? You've been in a coma for over a year and just woke up. Are you sure you're ready for that? Is your mom ready to let you go?"

"I don't care. I missed all that time. I don't want to miss anything else. We can figure something out."

"I would like that."

"We could get an apartment together. Or I could secretly live in your dorm or something."

"Well, I do have a roommate. We weren't sure if we were going to live on or off campus this year."

"Oh. Well if you already have plans with someone else," she looked down at her hands.

"Michelle, we can all live together."

"Really?" She looked back up at me.

"Yeah! Stefanie is really awesome. You'll love her."

"Are there any cute boys in Brookhaven?"

"Oh yes. You'll have to meet Andrew."

"Oh! Who's Andrew?"

"You have to see him to believe him. Tall, dark, handsome, gorgeous."

"The total opposite of someone we know."

I laughed at this. Michelle seemed to be as over Josh as I was. And I was not at all jealous of her reaction to Andrew. I think I needed a break from boys. Josh had consumed my mind for far too long.

"I better get back or my mom will have a conniption fit."

I watched Michelle walk away back down the road toward her house. I longed to follow her. Her mom would probably bake her cookies, or brownies or something and they'd sit and talk for hours about nothing. Jealousy rang through me. All I ever wanted was a relationship that wasn't broken, someone on my side who I could depend on.

I shuffled down the road to my house slowly. I had no idea if Josh was still there. I wanted him to be and at the same time, I didn't. Michelle was right, Josh was a good guy, and even if lying to me was a crappy move on his part, he was just trying to protect her, and me for that matter. Now I was armed with the truth as to why she'd been on the road that night. She was coming to see me. I guess if I dwelled on it long enough I could make the accident my fault, but really, it was just an accident.

When I'd turned on to the street that led to my house, I saw Josh's truck. He was still there. I stopped walking and watched my house. Josh paced back and forth between his truck and the porch. He opened the truck door then slammed it shut again. The sound resonated back to me. I closed my eyes and prepared myself for the conversation we'd have. I mean, I had no clue what I was going to say, but something needed to be said. Something.

Josh just wasn't the same boy I'd fallen for when we were kids. And all the 'what ifs' I'd thought about us were now irrelevant. We were just a summer fling and nothing more could come of it. He'd made that clear when he decided to be with Michelle. Again.

I walked on, each step reminding me that I needed to make a decision. I needed to leave town. One, because I had to go back to school and two, because there was nothing left for me here. My mother had left an indelible mark on this town and had included me in her fall out. I wasn't welcome here. I would always be known as Kim's daughter, I'd always be sought after by people looking for things I could not and would not give them. If Josh wanted to stay in this town, then I couldn't be with him. I know he said he wanted to stay with Michelle, but he needed to know that I wasn't coming back.

I was almost to his truck before Josh noticed me. He ran up to me and hugged me.

"Jenna, I'm so sorry. Please, can we talk?"

I didn't respond verbally, instead I nodded and continued to the house.

I surveyed the living room. I'd be leaving everything behind. I'd have dad sell the house and stay in Brookhaven next summer and every summer after that until I graduated and moved on. Maybe I'd move in with Andrew.

"Jenna," Josh said behind me. I hadn't turned around yet. He touched my arm and pulled me around to meet him. The familiar tingle of anticipation welled up inside me. Josh gripped my arm tighter so, I grabbed his and did the same like we needed to hold on to each other or we'd just fall away.

"Josh." I said his name like he'd said mine, full of hope and sorrow, and desire.

He grabbed the side of my face and neck and pulled me to him. His mouth met mine in a hard kiss. His tongue exploded into my mouth, pushing and caressing my own. I didn't fight against him, but melted into him. I let him wrap his strong arms around me and hold me. My hands traveled up his chest, over his collarbone and to his neck. I intended to push him away but I clung to him, pressing myself close to him. He snaked his arm around to my lower back under my shirt. I was lost in his mouth, but fully aware of his skin against mine. The hand on my face entwined in my hair, so when he gently tugged at the back of my neck, my head was pulled back, exposing my neck. I let out a small sound, a groan. Josh released my mouth and stared at me. His eyes were wild. He let go of my hair and before I knew what he was doing, he'd pulled off my shirt. I stood there stunned, staring at him, but not for long because his shirt was gone too.

I was double stunned.

I'd prepared myself for a break up conversation. But here was Josh, half naked in my living room, kissing me like he'd never kissed me before. I was internally conflicted. My body was screaming for him. I wanted my hands on his smooth, tight chest, I wanted his hands to roam over my back and pull me to him. But my mind said no, back away. And my heart. My heart was just sad and caught in the middle.

I stood there in just a white eyelet skirt that was grass stained from sitting in the grass with Michelle, and a white bra. Josh, in his dingy jeans and work boots looked like a farming god. His chest heaved with tension and desire for me. His earlier words about wanting to stay with Michelle were forgotten. He only had eyes for me and they were on me.

I took a few steps back and watched his eyes widen. His face grew sad until I extended my hand toward him. I had no idea what possessed me to do this, but as I watched, his eyes darkened and he smiled hungrily at me, all my determination to end us left me and all that was left was now. He took my hand and I led him back to my bedroom.

* * *

I woke up hot and sweaty and tangled in sheets and body parts. Josh's naked body parts, but I needed him off me, I was about to burst into flames I was so hot. He looked so peaceful though. The sun was just peeking through my curtains and cast a warm glow across his bare body. I was on my left side, and he on his right so we faced each other. He was still sleeping and snored lightly. I bet I could wriggle out from under his arm and leg. I sat up slowly, then drew each leg up to my chest. Once I was out from under him, I extended my leg over him to the floor. I hopped on one foot until I freed my other leg. Made it. Now what? Shower? Get dressed? Wake him up?

I stood there staring at him wrapped up in the soft pink sheets. This was a mistake. I needed to leave. I needed to leave him. Sleeping with him again was not the way to accomplish either of those things.

He stirred. I stilled.

"Jen?" he mumbled.

"Yeah."

He flipped over. The sheets caught on the bed and revealed every delicious inch of him. All of them.

"Yeah," I said again. My brain was frozen.

"Where are you going?"

"Yeah. Um…Nowhere. To the bathroom. To shower!" I shouted that last part.

"Can I join you?"

"No." I snapped out of my trance. "No. I'd like to shower alone, please."

"Okay." He gave me a questioning look while he adjusted the sheet and covered himself up. Like it did any good. Pale pink sheets hide nothing.

"I'm going to go now." And I skipped out of the room without waiting for an answer.

The hot water cascaded over me but it didn't bring any answers. I stood under the pounding spray a while before I did anything. I needed my head to be clear. I needed the image of his naked body out of my mind. I needed to stop replaying the night. Josh had clearly said that he wanted to stay with Michelle. But what we had just done, said so much more about his feelings for me. I sighed and snatched the soap and washed away his cologne, his sweat, and everything else of his. Clean body, clear mind, and broken heart.

When I was done I wrapped a huge fluffy towel around my body and went back into my room. Josh was still there but he'd put on pants. Good. That made it easier to talk to him. He was sitting on the edge of the bed with his elbows resting on his knees.

"Josh. We need to talk."

"I know."

"You do?"

"Yeah. I wanted to talk to you too."

Okay, this might go easier than planned. I sat next to him on the bed, but not too close. His cologne had an intoxicating effect on me and I'd lose my words easily. I doubt I'd be able to smell it on him after the night we had, but I wasn't taking any chances.

"Josh. I'm leaving in a few days."

"I know. That's what I wanted to talk to you about."

"Oh yeah? Why's that?"

"I want to come with you." He looked at me then. I could imagine the look on my face. Eyes wide, jaw open, chin on the floor. That was not what I was expecting to hear.

"I, um. Why? What about Michelle?" I had no clue what to say. He'd shocked me into silence.

"I don't know what I was thinking. I wanted to see your reaction I guess. I wanted to know if what we had was real. I thought you'd be happy about this Jenna. You don't seem to be."

He got up from the bed and stood in front of me. I felt small looking up at his chiseled features. He looked like Paul Bunyan or a non-green Jolly Green Giant. His stance was wide and his arms were folded across his bare chest. It wouldn't even the playing field if I stood up, he's still a head taller than me. But I did anyway. I wanted to look him as square in the eye as possible.

"Josh. I'm leaving by myself. Alone."

Josh dropped his arms and swiped up his t-shirt from the top of the dresser. He looked at me for a moment longer than stormed out of my room.

"Wait, Josh! Let me explain." I followed after him fully aware that I was still technically naked. I clutched the towel around me when I reached the living room. Thank God for curtains.

"No, Jenna. I get it. You don't want to be with me even though last night should have made it clear that you did. I'm hurt Jenna." He looked hurt as he quickly dressed himself.

"Yeah, well you were all ready to be with Michelle yesterday. You just suddenly changed your mind?"

"Well, yeah!" He said it like that kind of answer was satisfactory. It wasn't.

"You can't just change your mind."

"Why, Jenna? Why?"

"Josh, you lied to me in a pretty big way. Last night was supposed to be the end, but then you kissed me."

"Isn't that enough?"

"No."

His eyebrows raised and he let out a sigh. He didn't even look at me. He just turned around and walked out the door. I stood there in the middle of my living room still dripping from the shower, wrapped in a towel, and watched the first love of my life walk away.

I sagged to the floor, tears streamed voluntarily down my face.

CHAPTER TWENTY-THREE

The next couple of weeks flew by quickly. It was the middle of August and I was ready for school to start in September. Stefanie had found the perfect apartment for us. It had two bedrooms, one bathroom, and it was practically free. So, maybe it wasn't perfect, but it would work for us. Initially Stefanie was hesitant about Michelle joining us, but several phone conversations later, Michelle and Stefanie had become friends.

I hadn't heard from Josh since the morning he walked out of my house. I had sobbed on the floor in my towel for over an hour, not just about Josh, about everything. All the stresses of the summer had finally caught up with me and they all came pouring out of me after Josh had left. I knew from the beginning that he and I couldn't be together like he wanted, but I had let him into my heart, I'd let his words seep into my mind and cloud my judgment. He'd told me he loved me and it's what I wanted to hear, what I needed to hear after years of neglect and belittlement from my mother and others around me. For some reason I had needed validation from him, from someone in this town for me to find my worth, when really I should have found it within myself.

Andrew had always told me I was worth something, that I mattered, but I'd never believed him or took him at his word because he didn't know about my past. I had never told him, but now I needed to. He needed to know where I came from, how I grew up, and what had happened this summer.

After my sob fest, I threw my energy into packing and cleaning. I'd wasted the summer with Josh and I hadn't cleaned out the junk from this house like I'd promised my dad I would. So I boxed everything up that I wasn't taking back with me and set it out on the back porch. I finally cleaned out my mother's room. I didn't find any more drugs and I didn't keep anything I found in there. I needed no reminders of her or my past.

Once everything was out, I cleaned the house and packed my own things and shoved them into my car the best I could. Michelle and her things still had to fit somehow.

When Michelle and I had first told Mrs. Banks about our plan for Michelle to come to Brookhaven with me, she was completely against it. Michelle still needed to do physical therapy and needed regular doctor's appointments. Michelle countered with something her doctor had said about getting back to a normal routine. Mrs. Banks still insisted Michelle needed to stay here, but after numerous conversations with doctors and recommendations for doctors in Brookhaven, Mrs. Banks agreed that Michelle could get her GED online and start college at Brookhaven Community College in the spring.

Mrs. Banks and I had talked briefly about her husband's involvement with my mother. She never blamed me or thought of me as a bad person because of what my mother had done. She thought I was a good friend to Michelle and apologized for what the mayor had done to me. We had gone to the police along with Mrs. Riley and told them what we knew about the mayor and the drugs and about the sweaty man he'd sent to my house.

The sheriff we spoke to was receptive to our information and told us he had recommitted himself to this town and making sure all of its residents were safe and drug free. This town had seen enough of this kind of thing, and he was ready to put an end to it. He wasn't too keen on the fact that I had initially lied before when I said that I wasn't home when it was broken into, but he was willing to overlook it so that we could catch the guy who did it. I wasn't sure if the sweaty man pretending to sell me vacuums worked for the mayor or if he was just an innocent guy who got caught up in the mayor's business. I made sure to tell the sheriff that I didn't want any more innocent people to get in trouble because of my mother and the mayor. This was on them.

While Michelle was finishing packing and talking with her doctors again about the move, I decided to go down to Miller's and pick up some food for the road. I also wanted to talk to Lauren. I hadn't seen her or talked to her since the night she'd stayed at my house. I felt like we could have been friends if everything hadn't gone crazy. I wanted her to see her potential and not be stuck here in Riverview as a grocery store clerk for the rest of her life.

I pulled into the parking lot and jogged to the front door. It was still boiling hot out.

"Hey there," Lauren said when she saw me.

"Hey, how have you been?" I asked.

"Good," she replied.

"That's good." I wanted to ask her if she'd thought anymore about applying to cosmetology school, but since I hadn't talked to her for a few weeks, I didn't know if she'd taken my comment about it seriously.

"Yeah. Hey, guess what?" she asked excitedly.

"What?"

"I applied to that beauty school you told me about." She smacked her gum loudly and smiled at me.

"That's so great!" I said.

"Yeah. I got accepted with a scholarship and everything. I'll be starting in January next year. I thought it was a little soon to start next month."

"Lauren, that's so amazing!"

"Yeah, I guess. My mom wasn't too happy about it. I think she really did expect me to stay here forever."

"I'm sorry," I said.

"It's fine. But now I have to figure out where to live and find a job and stuff." She flipped her hair and switched the elbows she was leaning on.

Now I felt bad, I'd told Lauren to go apply for college and then completely ignored every other aspect of doing so. Going to college meant she had to leave Riverview and go off on her own to a new town where she knew no one except me. I was a terrible friend.

"I'm sorry Lauren. I should have helped you with all of this."

"No, it's okay. I can figure it out. I mean, Brookhaven has to have a grocery store, right?"

I chuckled a little. "Yes, several," I said, still laughing.

"Well then, there you go. I can work at one of them.

An idea suddenly popped into my head and before I could stop to think about it, I blurted it out. "Lauren! You should live with me, Michelle, and my roommate from last year, Stefanie. She just found a super cheap two bedroom apartment. I bet we could squeeze one more person in there."

"Are you serious?" Lauren placed both hands flat out on the counter and squealed with delight. "That would be so awesome," she exclaimed.

"Yeah," I said to myself. I really should have run this by Stefanie. She seemed to be okay with Michelle moving in with us. Besides, one more person would make the rent even cheaper.

"Jenna," Lauren said. Her eyes had grown wide.

"What?" I asked.

"Um," and she pointed behind her.

I turned to look at what she was pointing at. There was a tall, thin man behind me, just staring at me. It was creepy. But the longer I stared back at him, the more familiar he became until it hit me. He was the sweaty man who attacked me in my house.

"What the heck are you doing here?" I said.

"I," he turned to leave.

"No! No, you don't get to leave. Not until I know who you are."

The man stopped before he got to the door and turned to face me.

"Who are you?" I asked.

"I just work for the mayor," he said. He was still backing away. He held up his hands like I was going to hurt him or something.

"That's not what I asked."

"Listen, I just needed money. My wife is pregnant and you know how jobs are in this town." He had begun to sweat profusely. "I just needed the money, I never meant for things to get out of hand."

"You work for the mayor?" I wasn't really asking him, more repeating his admission to myself. "He sent you to my house?"

"Yes, he told me to go to your house and pick up the two bags. He said I could keep one to sell and give him the other. I just needed the money," he said. He looked away from me, sweat continued to drip down his face and neck.

"What's your name?"

"Please, I don't want any trouble. I just needed the money," he said, still backing up toward the door.

"I don't want trouble either, but you ransacked my house and attacked me."

"I'm sorry," he pleaded.

"Just tell me your name."

"Ryan Lascoe," he said quietly before slipping out the door.

I looked around to see if anyone else had just witnessed that exchange, but there was no one in the store except Lauren and me. Why did I always meet people here that I didn't even want to see in the first place? It had all started with seeing Josh my first day back, then the mayor, and it just went downhill from then on. It's a good thing I wouldn't ever be coming back here.

"What was that all about?" Lauren asked.

"That was the guy who attacked me in my house the day you spent the night."

"Oh," she replied.

I paid for my food and went back home in a daze. Mrs. Riley, the sheriff, and I had been building a case against the mayor. Now that I knew the name of the sweaty man, assuming he'd given me a real name, we had almost everything we needed to bust the mayor.

I almost felt bad for Ryan Lascoe. He was probably some poor, lowly political worker who had gotten caught in the mayor's crosshairs. Ryan probably didn't even do drugs, he was just trying to provide for his family.

I called Mrs. Riley and Mrs. Banks and told them what had happened at the grocery store. I also phoned Stefanie to tell her about Lauren. I could hear the hesitation in her voice when she reiterated the size of the apartment to me five separate times. I assured her that everything would be fine and mentioned that the rent would be cheaper and how much we'd save on food, especially if Lauren did decide to work at the grocery store. Stefanie reluctantly agreed and I was finally ready to leave Riverview for good.

CHAPTER TWENTY-FOUR

The day had come for Michelle and me to leave. I grabbed the last box from the hideous couch and paused before I walked it out the front door. I was going to miss this couch, it had seen some of the best days of my life, but also held the painful reminder that I'd lost a best friend and the first, real love of my life. I had thought about bringing it with me, but I had no way of getting it there. I was also trying to keep with the theme of not taking anything that held bad memories with me from this place, only good ones. I'd left most everything in the house and took with me a few clothes, my quilt and the knick knacks I'd taken off my dresser and cork board at the beginning of the summer.

I stepped away from the car and looked down the road. A low rumble alerted me that someone was headed my way. Michelle. She and her mom pulled in behind me.

I really wasn't taking as much back with me and I had the whole back seat of my car open for her stuff. And she had a lot of stuff.

"Did you pack your whole room?" I asked as I walked around to the back of their car.

"Yeah pretty much," Michelle replied.

We started moving stuff to my car, boxes, suitcases, bedroom stuff. We squished her pillows in around our stuff and closed the trunk quickly. It was going to be interesting when we opened it after a five hour drive.

"You girls be careful, okay? Call me when you get to Brookhaven. I got Michelle a new phone," Mrs. Banks said as she hugged each of us. "Where's Josh? I thought he'd be here to see you two off." I looked down at my shoes awkwardly.

I'd told Michelle what had happened between Josh and me. She was supportive of me and we took turns calling him a jerk-faced douchebag and other immature insults. It didn't really accomplish anything, or even make me feel better about the situation, but we laughed about it together.

"He's not coming Mom, he was a jerk to Jenna the other day, so he's just not coming," Michelle piped up.

"Oh, well I'm sorry to hear that. I know you three used to be close." She gave us a sad smile and hugged us again.

"You take care of her okay?" Mrs. Banks said when she hugged me.

I felt bad taking Michelle from her so soon after her husband had left, but Renee was still going to be here and Mrs. Banks and Mrs. Riley were good friends.

To be honest, I had half expected Josh to be here to say goodbye, but the other half of me wasn't surprised that he wasn't. I'd sent him a text to let him know that I was leaving. I'm sure he and Michelle had talked at some point, but it would have been nice just to say goodbye to him.

With a few last hugs and goodbyes, Michelle and I hopped in the car and drove off down the dusty road and out of Riverview, forever.

Epilogue

Josh

The damned song was on the radio again, the one I'd been so adamant about making Jenna's and my song. The smallest thought of her brought all the memories I had of her flooding into my mind. God I missed her. I missed when she was mine. This song said exactly how I felt about her. I missed her next to me in my truck. I missed the way her perfume filled the cab and lingered after she was gone. I missed the way she fit so perfectly into my arms. I missed just being us on her ugly couch just watching movies. I missed us at the river. God, I missed the river. I hadn't been able to go there since she left.

I couldn't escape her. Not now that I finally understood what Jenna was talking about. This song wasn't a love song. It wasn't about two people falling in love, it was about two people remembering the time when they were in love, but were not anymore. Jenna was right.

I flipped the radio off, with my luck it would just be playing on another station. I turned down the old dirt road and floored the accelerator. Dirt and rocks kicked out from under the back tires, leaving a dust trail behind me. I was going nowhere fast, I just needed to get away, and I was going to the one place that would fill the void she created when she left. The river.

Jenna had always claimed the river as hers, but I liked to think of it as mine. It held a lifetime of firsts for me. The first time I caught a fish with my dad. My first time swimming. The first time I saw a girl naked; Jenna. The first time I kissed a girl; Jenna again. I lost my virginity here with Jenna, and this first time I fell in love. It amazed me how connected I was with Jenna and the river.

I skidded to a stop just before I would have driven into the water. I liked living on the edge like that. No, not really, but the rush of being so close to plunging my truck into the river was exhilarating. I hopped out and threw my shirt and shoes into the back of the truck and walked right into the river, letting shallow waves splash against me.

I let my hands skim the top of the water and closed my eyes as I walked further out into the river. I could almost feel Jenna beside me. I remembered the day we met here after her run in with the mayor. I'd known something was up, but I waited to let her speak. When she didn't, I moved closer to her and felt her respond to my touch. We'd been playing at the edge of something for a while now, but we'd always stopped before going too far. In that moment though, I wanted to go too far. I needed to. I couldn't stand to be that close to her and not go all the way. When she followed my lead, I took it and ran with it.

I didn't know the difference between just sex and making love, but I knew then that I was in love with Jenna. She made me feel complete, the way she laughed at my jokes, the way she touched me and kissed me, and made me feel wanted and needed. I needed Jenna this summer. I was desperate to hold on to her, to anything about her, anything she'd give me and she gave me everything.

It was a confusing time for everyone. Jenna being back, Jenna and I rekindling our relationship, then Michelle waking up. I didn't know what to think or do. I felt obligation to Michelle because we had been together right before her accident, but Jenna made me feel alive again after so many dark days.

I shook my head. I'd ruined everything. I hadn't listened to my heart. It had said, go with Jenna, she wants you while my head said, be with Michelle, she needs you. Jenna had said over and over again that she wasn't going to come back and that was what had made me turn away from her.

I dove under the clear, cool water and let the memories of the summer wash away from me. I didn't want to remember them anymore. Jenna and Michelle were both gone and I was left with nothing, only the memories of when we were us.

And now a preview of

Pieces of Me

Erica Cope

You expected to be sad in the fall. Part of you died each year when the leaves fell from the trees and their branches were bare against the wind and the cold, wintery light. But you knew there would always be the spring, as you knew the river would flow again after it was frozen.

-Ernest Hemingway

PROLOGUE

"Where are we going?" Sean asked for the fiftieth time since we left this afternoon but I wasn't about to ruin my little surprise. He always went all out for holidays, birthdays, and anniversaries and this anniversary was a big one. Well, to us anyway. So I planned something special for him as a surprise.

It was a gorgeous summer night here in the middle of Kansas. The full moon was high and the stars dotted the night sky. I had already called the hotel to let them know we'd be checking in late. I smiled to myself as I realized I had almost pulled this thing off. We were celebrating three-years together—which is a pretty big deal when you're only eighteen.

"I told you, it's a surprise," I said, unable to stop the huge grin from forming. He knew I hated surprises, but that didn't stop him from torturing me every time an opportunity presented itself, so I was enjoying having the shoe on the other foot for a change.

"Come on, Aria. Give me a hint," he begged, and because I was a sucker, I couldn't resist.

"Oh, fine," I said with an exasperated sigh. "Reach back there and grab my purse. Your hint is in the envelope."   I tried to pretend I was irritated but really, I was just too excited and impatient to keep the secret from him any longer.

He smiled at me like a child who was just given a cookie after being told he couldn't have any dessert. I smiled back as he unbuckled his seat belt and leaned back to reach my purse from where I'd set it behind my seat.

As he picked up the envelope he looked over at me and said, "You know I love you, right?"

"Yes, I do."

CHAPTER 1

One Year Later.....

I knew the moment that I decided to come here that I am a complete and total masochist. It's not like I knew what movie would be playing, but I should have known that, even miles away, the tiniest thing has the ability to trigger memories. Memories that intensify the ache in my chest, the one that never really goes away, and cause it to expand and crush my insides until there's nothing left but pulp. There's no escaping that.

But what were the chances that they would be playing *that* movie? I wasn't expecting the latest blockbuster but I certainly wasn't expecting a movie that is several years old to be playing here tonight. I had been looking forward to this all week, since I first saw the flyer tacked to a telephone pole near my apartment.

Movies in the Park:
A contemporary version of the drive-in theater at a park.
Enjoy some of today's new releases and old favorites.
It's a wonderful way for the family to enjoy summer nights.

When I read the flyer a week ago, I thought it sounded so whimsical and fun—like something out of a movie—so I figured I would check it out and enjoy a much needed night out. I've been cooped up in my lonely apartment for nearly a month now with nothing to do but remember better days. But now that I'm here, I think I would have been better off staying in bed

"I can't do this," I mutter under my breath backing away from the large screen in the middle of the quaint little park. But just like a typical glutton for punishment, I can't tear my eyes away. All I can do is back away slowly with my eyes glued on the familiar opening credits. If I wasn't so wrapped up in my inner turmoil I would have remembered that despite how alone I may feel on a regular basis, the park is currently full of other movie-watchers and that I really need to pay attention to where I am going.

I back into what feels like a brick wall with an 'oomph' as the breath is knocked out of my chest and my Coke and extra-buttery popcorn spill down the front of my white blouse.

I make some really intelligent sound like, "Gah" as I turn to face the person I just so gracefully backed into.

"I'm sor—" My words are cut off by one of the most breathtaking smiles I have ever seen. Six feet tall, with wavy blonde hair that hangs casually over his eyes and the brightest blue eyes I've ever seen smile down at me, clearly amused by my disheveled appearance.

Or maybe it is the fact that he can clearly see through my soaked shirt.

"Well hello," the stranger says.

"I'm, uh, sorry."

"It's okay. You clearly were distracted," he smiles kindly. "Not the chick flick you were hoping for?" He gestures toward the large screen, reminding me why I was making my escape in the first place.

"Um, no, I just remembered I had something to do," I stammer through the lie. "Sorry for bumping into you."

"Don't be sorry, I never would've had the courage to talk to you otherwise." The way he's smiling at me, laying it on real thick, makes it obvious that this guy has no trouble talking to the ladies. I roll my eyes and start walking past him.

"Wait!" He reaches for my hand to stop me and I immediately jerk it away as if he just shocked me. It doesn't faze him for long and despite my staring up at him with wide-eye confusion like a crazy person, he tries again. This time, instead of reaching for my hand, he holds his out to me and says, "I'm Holden."

I look down at his hand and then back up into those crystal blue eyes. I know the proper etiquette requires me to shake his hand and introduce myself in return but I can't get the words out. Then I hear the opening line from the movie behind him and, just like that, my world shifts. I forget how to breathe and suddenly I'm no longer standing here in the middle of the park. I'm fifteen again, sitting in a dark theater on my first real date. Sean smiling nervously at me, so embarrassed, as our hands brush up against each other in the large bucket of popcorn we were sharing.

My heart constricts painfully as I snap back into reality. I can't be here anymore. I have to get out of here. It's just too much.

Why did it have to be *that* movie? Why couldn't I just have one night where my thoughts weren't absorbed in painful recollections?

And then the guilt comes crashing down on me for even wishing that it didn't hurt so much—of course it hurt. I *should* hurt. It's my fault he isn't here anymore. I should feel this pain every day for the rest of my life. I deserve it.

With one last look at Holden's outstretched hand, I walk away throwing the now empty cup and bucket in the trash. My skin feels sticky from the soda and butter that has soaked through my shirt— I should have just stayed in tonight.

As I unlock my bike from around the old maple tree that I'd tied it up to not even twenty minutes ago, I can't help but look back at where I left Holden hanging. He is staring at me, confusion written all over his face. He probably isn't used to girls being so rude to him. I feel bad for brushing him off, but I can't stand to be at this park any longer. It's not like I'm ever going to see him again anyway.   I pedal quickly on the way home and my legs burn in protest but I make it back to my one bedroom apartment within minutes. There isn't a bike rack available and no trees nearby so I carry my bike up the two flights of stairs to my apartment like I have every day for the last month. Yes, I've been here an entire month and the first time I try to do something semi-social I regret it. I'm thinking that's a sign.

I lean my bike against the wall in the doorway. The apartment is boring with plain white walls and tan carpet. There is one large window in the living room overlooking the parking lot below and another small window above the kitchen sink. There's one tiny bathroom in the short hallway between the living room and my bedroom. There's another window in my bedroom but that is it as far as natural lighting goes which, I suppose, is why the walls are white—a sad attempt to make the place seem brighter than it is.   It isn't anything fancy—which upset my mother more than I thought it should—but it is the closest complex to the campus which is of more importance to me since I don't drive. I haven't driven in over a year now and I'm not sure if I ever will feel comfortable getting behind the wheel again. Not after what happened....

I close my eyes and will myself to stop reliving that night over and over. I strip my clothes off leaving them scattered behind me on the floor as I head down the hall to my tiny bathroom, turning the shower all the way on hot. The scalding water burns away all feeling on the outside of my body but does nothing for the pain I still feel on the inside, the kind of pain that settles in your chest and makes a home there.

I remain in the shower until the water runs cold and even then I can't seem to make myself get out. Something about the water pounding down on me makes it easier to breathe.

It's not until my fingertips are wilted and my hands are turning blue that I finally feel numb enough to force myself to turn off the water. I dry off and instead of putting on pajamas like a normal person would, I pull his shirt off of one of my hangers. I'm careful not to look at the guitar or that damn cardboard box with the words 'Pieces of Us' written in black marker that rest on the floor of my closet. I shoved them both as far out of my view as I could manage in the tiny closet when I moved in, because I know I can't go there yet. So the box remains unopened, and the guitar untouched, and they both continue to taunt me. I quickly push the closet door shut to further hide them from my view. I don't want either of them here but my mom insisted that I bring the box and my dad insisted I bring the guitar. I think he is still hoping that someday I'll change my mind and play for him again. I don't want to disappoint him, but at the same time, I never knew it was possible to hate inanimate objects this much.

I lift the collar of his shirt up to my nose only to be disappointed that it's starting to smell less like him and more like me. I cross the room and open the drawer to my nightstand, frantically pushing everything aside to find what I'm looking for. I locate and pull out the half-empty bottle of his favorite cologne. I'll have to get some more soon. I spritz it generously all over his shirt, finally inhaling the comforting yet heart-breaking scent before curling up on my side under the covers.

As I lay there inhaling the clean crisp scent of him, I think to myself that yes, I really am a masochist, torturing myself like this but it's the only piece of him I have left.

I set the alarm on my cell phone and notice a text message and a couple of missed calls—all from my mom. I don't respond. I can't deal with her right now. She'll want to talk about it and that's something I'm still not ready to do. The psychologist in her reminds me daily that talking about what happened is a crucial part in the grieving process—blah, blah, blah.

I didn't want to think about The Five Stages of Grief and how I'd been stuck on stage four for much longer than mom thought was healthy. I just didn't want to hear any more about it from her.

Tomorrow I start my freshman year of college—a year later than I was supposed to and all alone. I still can't believe that my life is turning out so different from what I was expecting. Sean should be here with me. But he isn't. All I have left is an old faded t-shirt and a box on the floor of my closet I can't bear to look at because it contains memories of the boy I love.

Pieces of Me by Erica Cope is now available!

ACKNOWLEDGMENTS

Mitchel Diemer
For putting up with my crazy. I love you
Erica Cope
For your initial and continued encouragement. I never would have done this without you.
Michelle Rowe
Thank you for believing in me when I didn't believe in myself. I believe in you.
Komal Kant
Thank you for your amazing ability to always stay positive and keep me going when I didn't think I could.

ABOUT THE AUTHOR

Heather Diemer is a Midwest girl who lives in the in the picturesque Flint Hills of Kansas with her husband and two children. If she's not reading or writing, or thinking about reading or writing, you can find her outside with her camera capturing the beauty of everything around her.

You can find Heather on Facebook. https://www.facebook.com/HDAuthor or on twitter at @heatherforreal

34845831R00117

Made in the USA
Charleston, SC
19 October 2014